Too Late For Escape?

He reached out and yanked her numbed figure against him. "We have a perfectly good marriage certificate and I'm damned tired of playing games. If I stay, there'll be a good deal of this . . ." He bent over and kissed her hard while his hands moved deliberately, caressingly down from her shoulders to her hips. "Now what's it to be? Do I go or stay?"

Krista stared dazedly up at him. Where had she gotten the idea that Ryan didn't know how to handle women?

Now . . . if he'd just tell her he loved her as much as she loved him . . . they'd solve everything!

Surrender My Love

by GLENNA FINLEY

The maiden who listens . . . is halfway to surrender.

—de Montluc

A SIGNET BOOK

NEW AMERICAN LIBRARY

TIMES MIRROR

SIGNET, SIGNET CLASSICS, SIGNETTE, MENTOR AND PLUME BOOKS
are published by The New American Library, Inc.,
1301 Avenue of the Americas, New York, New York 10019

FIRST PRINTING, JANUARY, 1974

    1 2 3 4 5 6 7 8 9

PRINTED IN THE UNITED STATES OF AMERICA

Chapter ONE

The car ferry *Ibn Batuta* which wallowed through Mediterranean waters between southern Spain and Morocco was hardly an inspiring sight.

Krista Blake decided that five minutes after the ferry left the quay in Malaga. She also decided that as a place to spend a honeymoon, the *Ibn Batuta* was definitely scraping the bottom of the matrimonial barrel. Now, after five hours on it with the buildings of Tangier just becoming visible through the haze on the coastline, she was doubly sure.

There were only two outstanding features on the *Ibn Batuta*: its name which came from an Arab hero of the Middle Ages and the kitchen ventilating fan which ruthlessly provided the hapless passengers with previews of meals to come. First, there was a breakfast aroma of chicory coffee—later came the fragrance of garlic-smothered chicken heralding lunch.

Since the usually placid Mediterranean had been turbulent during the crossing, the kitchen fan had served a twofold purpose . . . only three passengers left the fresh air on the uncovered decks for the reeking confines of "Le Snack Bar" at the stern.

Krista was one of them. Another was the tall man stretched out in a flimsy deck chair a few feet away. He was calmly ignoring the program of

5

Arab music blasting from a tinny speaker over his head as he kept his attention on the paperback he was reading.

Krista frowned as she surveyed him. It wasn't fair that anyone should look so unruffled after five hours on the *Ibn Batuta*. Her lips twisted in a grimace of displeasure. If just once Ryan Talbot would join the human race and fray at the seams like other mortals!

But he hadn't—not since they had left New York three days before to fly to Spain. He had stepped off the plane seven hours later at Madrid's Barajas Airport looking like a man who had fully enjoyed a good night's sleep—which of course ... he had. Krista, on the other hand, hadn't managed to close an eye during the flight and jet-fatigue gave her complexion a translucent quality usually found only on plague victims in their final hours.

Ryan had taken a startled look at her and called a taxi with an imperative gesture. A half hour later he delivered her to their adjoining hotel rooms and saw that she was horizontal before she started gibbering. Then he had happily gone out to visit the Prado Museum for the rest of the day.

He had maintained the same careless "watch-dog" attitude on the Talgo express to southern Spain. The switch to trains had come about when Krista flatly declared she'd rather walk to Morocco than climb into another airplane.

Ryan had merely nodded calmly at her outburst and seen to their tickets. Hours later, he unearthed the only cruising taxi at the station to take them to the hotel in Torremolinos. Fifteen minutes later when Krista was falling into bed—a discreet knock at the door had revealed a room service waiter bearing tea and toast. "From Señor Talbot," he had announced.

If Krista hadn't been so thirsty, she would have pounded on the locked connecting door to Ryan's room and announced that such first aid wasn't necessary. As it was, she drank every drop of tea and scrounged the last crumbs of toast.

Such omnipotence didn't endear the man to her, however, and now—when she was trying to keep her stomach from imitating the *Ibn Batuta*'s heaving decks, she almost hated him.

Krista scowled and stared down at the waves by the side of the *Batuta*'s green hull. As she did, the skin on her forehead prickled and she rubbed it absently.

"If you don't get out of that sun, you're going to be burned to a crisp," came a calm masculine pronouncement behind her.

Krista turned to face the deck chair again and surveyed Ryan's lean figure in cotton slacks and short-sleeved shirt balefully. His sleek brown head remained bent over the book in his lap. "I don't see *you* moving," she announced.

"I'm not a blonde who's practically a redhead." He did look up then and met her gaze squarely. "You'd better go find a hat."

"The only hat I have is locked in my suitcase down in the bilge or wherever they took it. Besides, I'm perfectly all right."

Ryan pulled his sunglasses down to peer over the top of them. "Maybe—but your nose is red already. I'd get under cover if I were you."

Krista tried to peer at the feature in question and merely succeeded in looking cross-eyed in the attempt. She wrinkled her nose experimentally and knew with a sinking feeling that he was right again.

"Not only that," Ryan continued, "if you get too much sun, you'll feel rotten on the trip to Marrakesh. A mini-bus isn't the last word in comfort at any time, so you'd better take care of yourself."

Krista glared at him wordlessly and then reluctantly moved to a patch of shade under the ventilating fan. As she saw Ryan's glance return to his book, she decided to renew the conversation.

"Wer'e coming into Tangier, you know," she said sweetly.

"Mmmm."

"Well, really!" The sweetness was slipping to an acid tone. "Aren't you even going to bother to go to the rail for a first glimpse of Morocco?"

"Something tells me it's safer here," he replied. "There isn't a life preserver on this deck and when you're in this mood, I don't want to get close to the rail."

"Very funny," she told him icily. When he didn't bother to respond, she went on in a virtuous tone which would have started an argument with an archangel. "I should think you'd be interested in seeing the country. After all, it was your idea to come here." She had the satisfaction of seeing his lips tighten at that.

"If I remember properly . . . you had a slight interest in the trip, too," he pointed out. "It wasn't entirely one-sided."

"Just because I showed some response then doesn't mean I feel the same way now. I still don't see why it was necessary to go to all this trouble for a month's trip abroad. You could have told everybody that I was accompanying you as your secretary or something. What was wrong with that?"

"They'd have thought we were having an affair.

That's what's wrong with it," Ryan said baldly, closing his book with a snap.

"Now you're being ridiculous and imagining things."

"Hardly, you're just being naïve. Zoo curators don't operate in the 'beautiful people' league. No affairs—no swinging swap sessions—we're the conservative, dull, reliable sort who just pay taxes—remember?"

She looked at him through half-closed lids, uncertain whether to take him seriously. Even in her angry mood, Ryan Talbot was a far cry from the "staid and dull" category. Over the past six months, Krista had watched too many women's faces brighten whenever he walked into the office they shared at the Woodsea Zoological Park and Botanical Gardens.

She was also aware that it was his lean six-foot frame rather than his enviable academic qualifications which accounted for the long list of feminine volunteers on their Children's Zoo project. The fact that Dr. Talbot remained interested only in the efficient operation of his zoo was a continual source of frustration to the females involved.

Krista had never bothered to enter the competition for the zoo director's attention. At the outset, she was too thrilled when he hired her as Nursery Director of the Children's Zoo to even think of her personal life. Later, she felt her dedicated attitude obviously pleased Ryan. He was in no mood for playful diversions at that point having just received his own promotion to Managing Director after the retirement of Dr. Baldwin, an internationally respected zoologist.

It was a quixotic gesture on Dr. Baldwin's part which had gotten them all in their current predicament, Krista decided. If the old zoologist hadn't been determined that Ryan be awarded this trip to confer with the directors of selected international zoos, she wouldn't be aboard a heaving Moroccan car ferry now.

"You're showing the effects of the sun already ... I'd better go down and unearth that hat for you."

Ryan's voice penetrated Krista's thoughts and she blinked, trying to come back to the present in a hurry. She shook her head decisively before he could get up from his deck chair. "I'm perfectly all right. Or, if I'm not—the sun hasn't anything to do with it," she countered. "So, don't change the subject." She leveled a finger at him. "All zoo directors who go on goodwill jaunts like this aren't married."

"You know how the invitation was worded." Ryan's gray-eyed glance held hers. "For the director of Woodsea Zoo and wife."

"That was because of Dr. Baldwin. They just didn't know he had retired."

"Granted. But even he acknowledged it was too late to change any arrangements by then. For pete's sake, Krista, why don't you give up? You know the score on this—we've certainly been over it enough since we left home. Don't forget, it was your big chance, too." He stared at her as if daring her to dispute the facts. When she stubbornly remained silent and turned her gaze toward the approaching shoreline, his jaw firmed in annoyance. Despite the attractiveness of her slim figure in the North African sunshine, he'd liked to have turned her over his knee at that moment and smacked her hard. Then maybe she would have shed the barrier of cool disdain she'd erected between them ever since they'd left home. He stirred uneasily in his chair—not knowing how to deal with this new Krista and wishing that he could have the old one back in her place. For despite her belief that he'd paid no attention to her since she'd arrived at Woodsea, she would have been surprised to know how carefully he had appraised her over the months.

Not only that—he'd liked what he had seen. The bright sandy hair that shaped her head so neatly, the soft delicate lips that could mold themselves to catch any man's glance, and even the violet-blue eyes which fairly glowed when she was bubbling with enthusiasm over one of her Children's Zoo projects.

Ryan's glance went over her once again and he sighed to himself. For the past few days, those eyes had been surveying him as dispassionately as a moldy specimen on a microscope slide to be assessed, dissected, and then thrown away. Which was a hell of a way for any twenty-four-year-old female to regard a man, Ryan decided irritably.

"Other people have affairs," Krista went on as if there hadn't been an interruption to their conversation.

"Well, I don't!" Ryan's patience deserted him. "Or if I did—I wouldn't pick a woman where I work—and I damned well wouldn't invite her on a study trip to North Africa and Europe to meet a bunch of colleagues. Give me credit for some sense. . . ."

"That's a silly way of looking at it!"

He said through clenched teeth, "Don't be more of an idiot than usual, Krista. Who's being illogical now?"

"I didn't say you were illogical. . . ."

"Then that's the only adjective you missed in describing my character over the past three days." The sound of a tug hooting by the *Ibn Batuta*'s stern made him thrust his paperback into the pocket of his sport jacket which was hanging on the deck chair and get to his feet. "C'mon ... we might as well change the subject and have a look at the scenery. As you said, that's what we're here for."

The weary resignation in Ryan's voice got through to Krista's conscience, making her acknowledge that she had been taking a perverse feminine delight in ruffling his composure. She didn't stop to analyze why but it *did* pass through her mind that the feeling was a new one; their relationship before this trip had been amiability itself. Ryan had treated her like an indulgent elder brother most of the time—when he had bothered to acknowledge her presence at all in the past. Their shared social life had consisted of a few placid business lunches and monthly zoological dinners which fell in the "duty" category.

"What's the matter?" Ryan glanced at her over his shoulder. "Don't tell me you're allergic to Moroccan scenery as well as to me."

"Certainly not." She moved slowly over beside him at the rail. "I was just thinking that I'd never seen you so annoyed before." She put up a hand absently to brush her hair back from her face as brisk coastal breezes swept along the *Batuta*'s open decks when the ferry headed in toward the breakwater.

Ryan made a self-conscious grimace and rubbed the back of his neck. "That makes two of us, then —we're both acting like bears with sore heads today. If we'd managed a little more sleep last night, things would look better. That damned hotel of ours must have attracted every motor scooter in Spain," he went on bitterly. "At three A.M., it still sounded like Memorial Day weekend on the Pennsylvania Turnpike. Just wait until I get my hands on that travel agent!"

Krista looked superior. "I had doubts about him when he took us to lunch and finished three martinis before his hamburger."

"That's ridiculous. I've known Howie for years," Ryan retorted irrationally. "Everybody's entitled to slip up once in a while." He scowled at her. "Just being in charge of the Children's Zoo doesn't give you the right to psychoanalyze my friends and criticize their personal habits. . . ."

"You'd have had more sleep last night if I had," she said smugly. "Howie chose the hotel."

"Then I'll complain when we get home. Right now I'd appreciate your remembering that I've tucked myself into bed for thirty-two years without help. Just because I lost some sleep in a Spanish hotel room because of a freeway under the window doesn't mean that . . ."

"*Perdóname*, señor." A harried-looking ship's officer clutching a typewritten list paused beside them at the rail. "This is the final check on passengers' passports. I must give the list to the Moroccan authorities as soon as we dock. May I have your name, please . . . ?"

"Talbot. Ryan Talbot." Ryan leaned over and stabbed at the list. "There it is. Right there."

"Ah, *sí*. El Doctór Talbot." The official made a check opposite the name and turned to Krista. He took time for an admiring perusal before saying, "And you, señorita?"

"Blake. Krista Blake," she responded automatically.

"Blake . . ." He ran his pencil down the list once and then again before he looked up, frowning. "I'm sorry, señorita. There must be a mistake."

"That's right," Ryan cut in wearily, "but it's not yours. Try Talbot. Mrs. Krista Talbot."

"*Seguramente . . . aquí está.*" The ship's officer was frankly bewildered. His glance went suspiciously between them. "Your wife, señor?"

"My wife," Ryan confirmed. "Mrs. Talbot forgets sometimes."

"Oh *ho.*" Comprehension lightened the officer's expression as he noted Krista's flushed cheeks. "I should have known. Newlyweds—as you say. A girl of my country would not be allowed to forget." Nudging Ryan obtrusively, he added, "You must help her remember, señor."

"We've only been married three days. . . ."

Ryan's declaration didn't faze the Spaniard. "Then you still have plenty of time, and what a pleasant task! My congratulations."

Ryan noted approaching storm signals in Krista's face. Before she could comment, he said, "You must have many other people on your list, señor—and I see they're about to lower the gangway. Don't let us keep you."

The other gave a guilty start. "You're right, Dr. Talbot. Please have both your passports ready when you disembark." He nodded absently and hurried down the stern stairs to the lower deck.

"Honestly!" Krista exploded as soon as he was out of earshot. "For pre-Cambrian mentalities, he takes the cake!"

"Why? I thought he was darned decent about your 'absentmindedness.' It would have been a different reaction if I'd said you were my 'traveling companion.' Spanish men have a strict code of behavior."

She sniffed. "There wasn't anything different about the look in his eye. That's the same all over the world."

"You're hard to please," Ryan drawled. "Just because he wanted to tease a brand-new bride . . ."

"Temporary bride, if you don't mind—"

His tone became as icy as hers. "Should I have put that on the passport application? Mrs. Ryan Talbot. Issued for one month only. Not to be renewed."

"I don't need reminding."

"Then stop reminding me." He shrugged into his sport jacket and gave a cursory glance over the side of the ship. "If we keep fighting like this, no one will suspect us for a honeymoon couple. Let's declare a truce, for Lord's sake. The guide should be waiting for us down on the pier with the rest of the group and I'd just as soon not broadcast our personal affairs."

"I suppose you're right." Krista rubbed her fingertip over her brow, realizing that her skin was beginning to feel parbroiled already. "I'm sorry, Ryan. Honestly I don't know what's come over me since we left home." She shook her head. "From the way I've been acting, you'd think I was first cousin to a fishwife. Do other newlyweds go through all this?"

Ryan's stern expression softened at her words and he reached over to flick the end of her sunburned nose gently. "Damned if I know. Probably we're both suffering from stage fright. After all, we didn't have any rehearsal for the big event. When Dr. Baldwin and his wife had to cancel out, we only had a long weekend to . . ." His voice trailed off as he searched for the proper words.

Krista filled them in. "Get married and assure everybody that we'd been unofficially engaged all this time." She chewed on the edge of her lower lip. "That's why I feel like such a fraud. We'd scarcely looked at each other before."

"Well, we didn't hurt anybody," Ryan said stubbornly. "If we hadn't scheduled the wedding, those tickets would have gone a-begging and you know that this trip is a terrific chance for both of us. They're doing tremendous things in European zoo construction these days and I'm hoping that the garden displays in Morocco will give us some landscaping ideas for our safari section. Surely all that justifies disturbing our personal lives a little bit."

"More than a little. When I think of how pleased the Baldwins were ... and that elaborate reception by the staff ..."

"Forget it. By the time we get back, the fuss will be all over. You can quietly file for an annulment and nobody will think a thing about it."

Krista looked at him pityingly. "Say it again and sound convincing this time."

He shrugged. "Why look for trouble? Maybe by then we'll have decided we can't live without each other and the problem will be solved."

Her head came up. "Don't be ridiculous. People don't stay married when they're not in love. After a month, you'll be panting to be a bachelor again."

"I doubt it, but you'll probably fall madly in love with a Moroccan waiter. Over here, they snatch you up and carry you off to the edge of the Sahara." As she would have protested, he said, "Well, that makes about as much sense as your imaginings. Look, Krista, we agreed to act like two mature adults for a month, so there's no need to panic now. You lead your life—I lead mine. No interfering as long as we display a nice married front before strangers. We certainly haven't had any trouble with things so far, have we?"

"No," she granted reluctantly. "But I wonder if

Hamid is going to believe your story about our needing two hotel rooms every night."

"It doesn't matter what he believes—just what he does."

"That's what I mean," she persisted. "Don't forget, we'll be using reservations made for the Baldwins." Her pleasant contralto took on dry overtones. "Since they just celebrated their fortieth wedding anniversary, I doubt if they requested separate rooms."

"Stop looking for trouble—we'll take things as they come." Ryan was leaning on the rail watching their docking progress. "The porters are starting to come aboard now. We might as well go down amidships."

Krista nodded absently. "Tangier doesn't look very different from the rest of the world, does it?"

"Well—" He drawled the word. "I'd say it was definitely different from Cincinnati."

She shook her head impatiently. "I didn't think there would be modern cement docks with ships steaming in and out like crazy." She gestured toward the end of the pier. "That terminal down there looks brand-new. Even the houses on the hillsides look just like Spain in those neat white blocks. Sort of like row houses in Baltimore or Manhattan."

"What did you expect?"

She shrugged. "Well . . . something more exotic, I guess. Remember that old movie on television last month where they showed the Casbah?"

"Deliver me from females who expect everything to look like a Charles Boyer movie. So much for your scientific mind." Ryan took her firmly by the elbow and urged her toward the steps to the lower deck. As they mingled with the other passengers below, he murmured, "At least the citizens should be exotic enough for you. There's even a snake charmer at the foot of the gangway."

"Golly, you're right." She looked more cheerful. "Everybody must be coming out to meet the ship."

"Or their relatives." Ryan nodded toward the pier where family groups were enthusiastically greeting debarking passengers whose personal belongings were carried in baskets or flimsy suitcases belted in the middle with a piece of rope.

"What are those things they're wearing?" Krista asked, still hanging over the rail.

"Everything from chenille bedspreads to cotton sheets if you ask me."

"It's the women who specialize in bed linen," she decided after another look. "The men are decked out in that kimono garb with the pointed hood. Is that a djellabah or caftan?"

He grinned. "I'm a zoologist, not a costume designer."

"Yes, but if I know you—you've been absorbing facts about Morocco ever since we left home." She put her head to one side inquiringly. "I bet you a quarter that you know the answer."

"If I wanted to make money, I should plead ignorance." Then as she merely raised her eyebrows, he went on, "All right, Madame Talbot. For your information, they're djellabahs. Caftans are the same thing but a more deluxe model. They come in all colors." He frowned slightly as he surveyed the people on the pier. "Dirty white must be big this season in Tangier."

She nodded. "They look terribly hot in this weather. Sort of like wearing a tent in a steam bath."

"I suppose it's all right if you don't have very much on underneath." Ryan urged her along the rail toward the cluster of passengers who were showing their passports before going down the gangway.

"Yes, but most of those men at least have on trousers. You can see them sticking out under the hem of the djellabah."

"Remind me to keep you out of Scotland," he told her severely. "Curiosity about a djellabah's one thing—a kilt is quite another."

Krista grinned unrepentently. "Put it down to an inquiring scientific mind."

"Pure feminine curiosity . . . you're not fooling me. Better get your passport ready. The line's moving again."

Krista obediently pulled it out of her purse. "What about our luggage?"

"The bags are down on the pier already," Ryan said before handing his passport to the Moroccan Immigration official at the top of the gangway who carefully compared it with the *Batuta*'s list of passengers.

"*Merci*, monsieur." The passport was handed back quickly and, after a cursory look at Krista's, they were waved politely onto the gangway.

"Why French?" Krista wanted to know.

"Take a look at the signs by the customs shed." Ryan pointed to a direction board where instructions were repeated in Arabic, French, and English. "Something for everybody."

Krista stopped at the bottom of the gangway to read it thoroughly. "Good heavens, I'm glad I don't have to decipher the Arabic version . . . everything looks like worms."

"Evidently the French and Spanish left their mark when they occupied this part of the world, so communication shouldn't be too difficult," Ryan said. "It's a good thing, because my Arabic is just like yours."

"Totally nonexistent?"

"Exactly." He paused by the pile of luggage on the pier and then looked over his shoulder as he was hailed by a man hurrying toward them from the customs area.

"Dr. Talbot?" As Ryan nodded, he came up to them, breathing heavily from his haste. "Allow me to introduce myself. My first name is Hamid"—his tanned face split in a grin as he confessed—"and my family name is so long that I won't bother you with it. Let me welcome you to Morocco, Dr. Talbot. Our zoology people are delighted to have such distinguished visitors."

While he was shaking hands with Ryan, Krista had a chance to observe that their guide was much younger than her first glance had indicated ... probably in his early twenties. He was of medium height but looked slight next to Ryan's broad shoulders. Even the bulky djellabah of dark green wool trimmed with white braid on the front and hood couldn't enhance the other's slim build. Hamid's dark eyes were his most outstanding feature and they were framed by long lashes that any woman would have claimed happily. Dark brown curly hair was kept cropped close to his well-shaped head. Evidently long hair styles for men stopped at the Moroccan border, Krista decided.

Hamid must have felt her intent appraisal because he interrupted his greetings to turn and smile inquiringly at her.

Ryan spoke up. "Krista, may I present Hamid." He captured her hand casually before he added, "This is Mrs. Talbot."

Hamid's bow was discretion itself but the appreciation in his glance as it swept over Krista's lovely figure wasn't lost on either of them. She felt Ryan's grip tighten.

"My wife is a zoologist, as well," he told Hamid. "We're both looking forward to seeing your country as well as conferring with your officials."

Hamid's lashes went down and when he looked up again, his expression was both discreet and respectful. "It should be a great honor for all of us. Now, Dr. Talbot . . ."

"*Mr.* Talbot will do fine," Ryan said firmly.

"Of course . . . since you prefer it." Hamid was amiability itself. "If you and Mrs. Talbot will walk ahead to the customs section at the end of the pier, I'll find a porter and we'll bring your luggage along. I have our transportation waiting just beyond the barrier."

"Do we follow the crowd?" Ryan asked.

Hamid nodded and gestured ahead of them.

"Just a minute, please." Krista moved quickly over to their piled luggage and pulled a bulging nylon shopping bag from the middle of it. "I'll carry this." She shook her head when Hamid started to reach for it. "No, honestly, I'd rather. Things fall out of it otherwise."

"We'll see you at customs," Ryan told Hamid and fell into step beside her. He waited until the guide was out of earshot before he frowned and surveyed the bag she was clutching. "I've been meaning to ask you for three days what in God's name you're carrying in that thing."

Krista didn't have a ready answer. "It doesn't do much for my 'sophisticated traveler' image, does it?" she admitted.

"I'm not worried about that . . . I'm just curious."

"Well"—she peered into the open top of the bag—"there's half a box of cookies from that confectionery in Madrid, four paperback novels for reading . . . I always read in bed," she informed him absently. "Then there's an orange from lunch on the Spanish train . . . a bottle of cologne . . . a bottle of nail polish . . . I was afraid to leave them in my suitcase for fear they'd break . . . my camera and four rolls of film . . ."

Ryan started to chuckle. "Never mind. I'm sorry I asked."

"I wish the nylon wasn't so transparent. Actually I meant to get an airline bag in New York but there wasn't time."

"You'll be all right unless the orange rolls out when you put it down."

"The orange is tucked down in the corner and hidden in a candy bar wrapper."

Ryan shook his head. "I can see why you keep clutching the handle. You could cause a stampede if that stuff falls out."

"Don't worry. You don't have to carry it." Krista was wishing she'd taken time to find an airline bag, after all.

"Would you be happier if you had the evidence hidden in one of those baskets?" Ryan had pulled her to a stop in front of a sidewalk salesman who had his wares piled around him. He leaned over and selected a covered basket decorated with brown and beige straw flowers. "At least it matches," he pointed out as he held it against her dark brown nylon topcoat.

"It would be wonderful," she agreed, fingering the flower trim. "Nice thick straw to hide everything." Then she looked dubiously down at the salesman, who gave her a gold-toothed smile in return. "Do you suppose it's terribly expensive?"

"You go on along while I negotiate for it." Ryan turned her toward the customs shed and gave her a gentle push. "Women always deal better with customs officials than men do. Just shake your head if they ask any questions."

When he joined her at Hamid's mini-bus five minutes later, she triumphantly indicated their luggage which the guide was storing in the back of the van. "We're all clear. They hardly asked any questions at all. Oh, wonderful! You bought my basket," she exclaimed happily as he handed it over with a flourish. "Hamid would have gone back to bargain for it but I said you'd manage."

"It was scarcely a major transaction," Ryan admitted with a slanted smile, "but thanks for the vote of confidence."

"Hmmm." Krista was shifting the contents of the shopping bag to her new purchase. "You must let me know how much it was so that I can repay you." She was so intent on her task that she missed the bleak look which suddenly transformed Ryan's expression.

"Don't worry," he snapped. "I'll present a bill in triplicate when the month's over. In the meantime . . . watch it, will you." He indicated Hamid's figure a few feet away. "Most brides don't offer to go Dutch with their husbands."

Krista opened her mouth to protest and then subsided as Hamid slammed the back doors on the bus and came around to rejoin them. "I see you've started collecting souvenirs of Morocco," he told Ryan with a nod toward Krista's already-bulging basket. "Our Minister of Tourism will be delighted."

Ryan merely smiled and opened the front door

for them to get in. "Are we the first of the group to arrive? I understood that the party assembled in Tangier."

Hamid helped Krista up the high steps to the bus. "I've already collected two of them. They weren't anxious to wait in the sun while you completed docking formalities so they stopped off at a bar a few blocks away. An air-conditioned bar," he added hearing Krista's indrawn breath when the hot air of the bus's interior hit her. "As soon as we get moving, *our* air-conditioning system will start working," he assured them. "It's very hot for May this year."

She smiled faintly, wondering what had happened to the harbor breeze flirting round the *Ibn Batuta*. As she reached up to blot her forehead with a handkerchief, she realized that the sunburn on her face wasn't aiding her comfort. Thank heaven, she had on a sleeveless blouse.

Ryan had shed his sport coat by this time and folded it on one of the empty seats. He still looked cool and comfortable in his open-weaved sport shirt, Krista observed. It would have been nice if she could have opened as many buttons at her throat as he had. She sighed slightly and moved across the warm vinyl seat to be next to the window.

"Does it matter where we sit?" Ryan was asking Hamid.

He shook his head. "Most people change around as the days pass. There will be an extra seat in the bus this trip so we won't be crowded."

Ryan nodded and fitted himself in at the far end of the seat from Krista. With his long length, she noted that his knees were uncomfortably close to the seat in front of him.

"If you want to stretch out, you can move your

feet over here," she offered as Hamid closed the door and went around the front to crawl in the driver's chair.

Ryan grimaced. "Thanks, I may take you up on that later. The designer of this thing must have been a midget."

Hamid threw a sympathetic smile over his shoulder. "Or maybe a Moroccan, Mr. Talbot. We're not as tall as those of you from the Western Hemisphere. You've probably noticed that already." He nodded toward the groups of people who were walking up the shoulder of the street toward the center of the city. "There are no giants in our ranks."

They followed his gaze and watched pedestrians mingle casually between automobiles and the crowded local buses which emitted dense clouds of exhaust as they moved off. Occasional donkeys trotted by loaded with bulbous rattan baskets or their owners sitting in relaxed ease over the animals' hindquarters.

Hamid started the mini and drove past scattered buildings advertising steamship offices and customs brokers. There were a few run-down bars with metal tables and chairs on the curbside but they were mainly deserted in the stifling midafternoon heat.

Krista turned her head to stare as Hamid drove past a group of women on the edge of the roadside who were ambling toward town. "If I hadn't seen them, I wouldn't have believed it," she exclaimed.

"What's that, Mrs. Talbot?"

"Those poor souls wearing all those clothes in this heat. They must have about three layers from their ankles to their necks plus their head-coverings." Her gaze encountered Hamid's in the rear vision mirror. "I don't see how they stand it."

He shrugged. "It's custom here. You must remember, Mrs. Talbot—most of the women we'll be seeing are farmer's wives. They are still very poor even though some of the land is fertile."

"Why does a limited budget make them put everything they own on their backs at the same time? Especially in this weather."

Hamid looked amused at her vehemence. "I must ask one of my sisters the next time I'm home. If I were married, I would be more of an authority on such subjects. Isn't that right, Mr. Talbot?"

"Let's just say that my wife seems to have a preoccupation with the Moroccan native dress," Ryan drawled. "It's new to me, too."

His amusement made Krista struggle to defend herself. "I'm merely interested in the country," she said, trying for a touch of dignity. "Unfortunately, I didn't have time for background reading before we left. Perhaps I can get some books while we're here."

"Possibly"—Hamid sounded doubtful—"but most of our publications are in French or Arabic. If you're fluent in either of those . . ."

"I'll wait until I get home, then," Krista said, defeated.

"Naturally, I'll do my best to explain things as we go along," Hamid said as he braked gently and swung the bus to the right-hand curbing.

"I'm sure that will be more than enough," she assured him. "My husband"—would the time ever come when she could manage that word without swallowing first?—"my husband and I are looking forward to this tremendously."

The guide's relief was evident. He beamed and

reached for the door handle as he turned off the ignition. "Splendid! Now, I'll just go in and retrieve the other two members of the group."

"There's no need." Ryan spoke up. "They're waiting for you." He nodded toward the doorway of the bar where two men were moving purposefully toward the bus, carrying suit coats over their arms.

One of them was slight and dark-haired, with an intent look behind his thick glasses. He was comfortably dressed in seersucker trousers and an open-throated, short-sleeved white shirt with a black necktie folded casually in the pocket.

His companion was closer to Ryan's height or he would have been if he'd straightened from the comfortable crouch he adopted as he rolled along at the side of the other man looking like an amiable bear out for a stroll. His sandy hair was liberally sprinkled with gray which appeared almost platinum in the sunlight and thick eyebrows projected from a broad forehead. The lines in his tanned face put his age closer to forty than thirty as first appearance suggested. His powerful shoulders were easily discernible under his thin dark-blue nylon sport shirt and, like his companion, he was wearing a pair of seersucker slacks.

Ryan got out of the bus as they approached and shook hands when Hamid made hasty introductions.

"Mr. Talbot, this is Mr. Freeman," he said, indicating the shorter man, "and Mr. Snow." He smiled charmingly toward Krista. "Mrs. Talbot— Mr. Freeman, Mr. Snow."

The bear broke away to offer a paw through the window and shake Krista's hand enthusiastically. "This is a real pleasure. I was disappointed when I heard the Baldwins couldn't make it but now I can see there are compensations."

"Do you know the Baldwins well?" Krista asked, overwhelmed with his enthusiasm.

"Met them in Vienna two years ago on a junket like this. I'm with the State Department." His eyes under their bushy eyebrows swung back to Ryan. "Public relations is my line. Incidentally, forget the Mr. Snow part—my name's Jeff." He jerked his thumb toward his companion. "This is Herb. Herb and I have been making a survey of Moroccan beer while we were waiting for you."

Herb Freeman spoke for the first time. He hiccuped gently and then pushed his sunglasses up on his nose. "It was quite an extensive survey." His voice was querulous and prim. "Your ferry must have been late docking. The others will be wondering what happened to us."

Hamid looked at him with some distaste. "We're ready to go as soon as you and Mr. Snow get in."

"Humph," the other snorted. "That can't be too soon for me. This heat would fry your brains."

From the care with which he was enunciating, Krista gathered that the beer-sampling session had affected him more than Jeff Snow, who was calmly following the smaller man into the bus. She waited until they were settled on the seat in front of her and Hamid had pulled away from the curb before she asked, "Who else are we going to pick up?"

Jeff answered before Hamid had the chance. "Just three more—the Westons . . . he's in Public Health in the States and Eve Lenz."

"Then there are going to be other women along?" Krista sounded relieved.

"Oh, yes," Hamid hastened to assure her. "Mrs.

Weston and Miss Lenz make the numbers almost even."

"My wife couldn't come," Herb Freeman put in unexpectedly. "She doesn't think these junkets are worth anybody's time or money."

There was a startled silence while Hamid frowned and the rest of the passengers searched frantically for something diplomatic to say. Krista was still frozen when Freeman turned to look at her over his shoulder and closed one eye in an elaborate wink. "That's what she told me after I told her that our budget wouldn't stand it."

There was an almost audible sigh of relief from the others as they realized Freeman was indulging in heavy humor at their expense.

"What did you say then?" Krista wanted to know.

"That she could join me in Cyprus after this jaunt. That's the only way she'd let me have my passport back again. Never marry a woman from the Bronx . . ." he told Jeff. "No sense of humor."

"I'll remember that."

Herb turned back to Krista. "Maybe you can help me. I promised I'd take back one of those Moroccan bird cages for her." He saw her puzzled expression and went on to explain. "They're about two feet tall . . . made out of twisted wire and painted white. Let me know if you see one in the shops, will you?"

Krista's eyes gleamed with interest. "I'd be glad to. They sound marvelous. . . ."

"No," Ryan said.

She turned her head. "What do you mean? . . . no?"

"You can't have one. Don't forget we still have to move around the Continent for three weeks after Morocco." He folded his arms across his chest. "A straw basket ... yes. Bird cages ... no."

Jeff's laughter rumbled. "That's what I like to hear in this day and age—masculine authority. I thought it had disappeared with the dodo bird and the tyrannosaurus. Who knows—I might take another look at the matrimonial state."

"Wait a while," Krista advised, as she shot a resentful glance in Ryan's direction. "Things aren't always what they seem."

"You mean if I see you dangling a bird cage from your finger one morning," Jeff persisted, "you've struck a new blow for womanhood?"

"If Krista appears with a bird cage one morning," Ryan answered before she could reply, "it merely means that she'll be the one to carry it. All the way home," he finished definitely. Then he gestured toward the buildings in front of them. "This looks like the newer section of town. That's an impressive beach in front of those luxury hotels."

"Very nice," Hamid confirmed, "but it's still too cold for swimming at this time of year. The wind is strong a good part of the day."

"We're not staying in Tangier, are we?" Krista asked.

Hamid shook his head. "We'll drive on to Fez today and spend the night there. Just now, I'm stopping at the Rif Hotel to pick up the rest of our party before we get on our way." He made a right turn and after a half block, swung left again to pull up in front of an imposing hotel facing the beach. As a uniformed bellboy wearing a red tarboosh on his head came hurrying out to the bus, he shut off the ignition and opened the driver's door. He snapped a few sentences of Arabic at the teen-ager, who nodded and headed back toward the lobby again.

"I'd better go along with him to make sure they have all the luggage," Hamid explained to the others. "Would you like to come in or would you rather wait in the bus? I won't be long," he added.

Ryan looked inquiringly at Krista, who shook her head. "We'll wait here, thanks," he told Hamid.

"I'm comfortable," Jeff Snow offered.

"Well, I'm not," Herb said, opening his door and clambering down on the sidewalk. "Be back in five minutes," he announced and strode purposefully toward the hotel lobby.

Hamid smiled and followed him.

Jeff watched them go and then leaned comfortably back in the seat. "Something tells me that things aren't going to be dull this next week. We'll have a real mixed bag on the tour." He grinned to take the sting from his words. "Maybe you've been briefed?"

" 'Fraid not. We only made our plans at the last minute," Ryan told him without looking at Krista.

Jeff didn't appear to find anything strange in the admission. "That happens all the time. It's a real struggle arranging these junkets."

"How did you get started in this line of work?" Krista asked.

"I must be classified as a den father on my civil service rating." Jeff's smile broadened. "Actually, my department handles all these invitations from foreign governments. On this particular trip, you and your husband represent American zoologists. The Westons are Public Health people ... or at least he is. You'll soon discover, though, that it's hard to keep his wife out of anything." He sighed and went on. "Herb Freeman's a little unorthodox—but OK when you get to know him."

"What's his line of work?" Ryan asked.

"Hospital administration . . . and damned good at it, too, I'm told. On this trip, he'll be teamed with Eve Lenz. She's a pediatric psychologist, visiting some of their children's services."

"Then we're an all-American party?"

Snow shifted uneasily on the seat before shaking his head. "Not quite. Miss Lenz lives in the U.S. now—but she's originally from Vienna. I understand she's just applied for American citizenship. Delia Weston is a naturalized citizen as well. Luther met her in Europe when he was with our occupation troops after the second world war. From the way Delia acts at times, you'd think she was a member of the D.A.R. instead of a first-generation American." He grimaced. "We'll have to watch our step."

Krista smiled at that. "Are you stationed in Washington, D.C., Mr. Snow?" At his pained look, she said—"Jeff."

"That's better. Nobody stays formal on a tour unless Delia hangs onto her dignity," he assured her. Then, answering her question, "Most of the time I'm in the Capital. It's a terrible place for a transplanted Californian." He glanced casually at the deserted sidewalk. "Morocco reminds me of southern California. That's not strange, I guess, when you remember they're similar geographic types."

"It looks more like Baja California to me," Ryan said, "with their luxury hotels right next to those scrubby vacant lots." He nodded toward the beach front. "The real estate promoters in this town still have their work cut out for them.

I must admit, though, that some of the hotels look plush."

"I've stayed in one or two," Snow said. "You're lucky if all the plumbing works. A state of affairs which isn't limited to Tangier," he added ominously.

Krista's eyes widened at his frank comment but before she could say anything, she saw the rest of their group emerge from the hotel.

A middle-aged couple was in the lead, talking to Hamid as they approached the bus. They looked like the caricature of American tourists . . . the man with a visored cap over thinning gray hair, short-sleeved synthetic shirt and polished cotton slacks. Canvas shoes with thick rubber soles completed his garb except for an expensive-looking camera hung around his neck. His wife was in a striped green and white jersey dress with a cardigan slung over her arm. Her graying hair was pulled back in a bun on her long neck and sunglass lenses were clipped onto her thick glasses. She wore a pair of serviceable walking shoes and the big leather purse hanging from her shoulder was large enough to hold provisions for a six-month stay.

By the time she reached the bus, Ryan had the door open to help her in.

Apparently his assistance wasn't needed. She slipped the purse from her shoulder and slung it along the seat, climbing inside with an economy of movement that Krista wished she could emulate. Only then did she turn to Ryan and offer her hand in a direct masculine manner. "How do you do, Dr. Talbot; I'm Delia Weston." She glanced over her shoulder. "Luther . . . let Hamid take care of that luggage. Come along and meet the Talbots." Turning back, she bestowed a wintry smile on Krista. "How are you, my dear. Terribly hot this afternoon, isn't it? Oh, Hamid, put that bottle of mineral water where we can reach it, please." Without waiting for an answer, she moved along the seat to allow her husband to crawl in beside her after he'd shaken hands with Ryan and given Krista a perfunctory nod.

"How do you do, all." He settled beside his wife and pulled off his cap to fan himself with the visor. "My God, let's get going so there'll be some breeze. What are we waiting for now?"

"The rest of our party," Hamid said with asperity, checking the hotel doorway. "It shouldn't be long. Oh, here they are. . . ."

Herb Freeman had appeared at the side of a tall brunette in her early thirties who towered over him by at least three inches. The disparity in height didn't appear to bother either of them. Mere inches or years didn't matter when a woman was as beautiful as that, Krista decided. All Miss Lenz needed was an apple to grace her own Eden.

Eve had a camellia complexion which was framed by lustrous straight black hair falling just below her shoulders. Her look of sleek sophistication was heightened by her slim, high-fashion figure and this, in turn, was elegantly set off by a clinging navy blue tunic over white slacks. White sandals with thick cork soles showed her disdain of extra inches as she strolled toward them.

Krista soon found Herb wasn't the only male to be affected by her presence. Jeff slid gallantly out of his place and onto the sidewalk as they approached, even managing a jerky bow. Ryan didn't turn around until the last minute so Krista was given a full view of his suddenly raised eyebrows and his admiring grin as the vision extended her hand.

"So you're Ryan Talbot." Eve's voice matched

the rest of her. It was pleasantly accented with the texture of thick cream. "This is a real pleasure for me."

"Miss Lenz," Hamid muttered unnecessarily from the sidelines.

"How do you do," Ryan said, making no attempt to remove his hand from Eve's clasp.

"I'm so delighted that you're with the group," she continued. "Actually I'm just a frustrated zoologist at heart. I hope you'll let me accompany you on some of your inspection tours."

"Why, of course. . . ."

"Possibly I can even contribute something. You know, I was a consultant on the staff of the Vienna zoo before I moved to the States."

Ryan's expression changed from mere admiration to definite interest. "I'd like to hear about that Safari-park of theirs. They've had a lot of publicity."

"Perhaps in the bus. . . ." Hamid put in significantly.

"Oh, of course." Eve removed her hand from Ryan's grasp lingeringly. "I didn't mean to keep you all waiting. Maybe you can sit next to me, Mr. Talbot. Or may I call you Ryan . . .?" As she stepped into the bus, she apparently noticed Krista for the first time. "Good heavens, I didn't know we had another newcomer. . . ."

"Krista"—Ryan interrupted hastily as he got in behind her—"may I present Eve Lenz. Dr. Lenz—this is Krista Blake. . . ."

His words were out and hanging in the air before he became aware of his gaffe.

Krista's cheeks went scarlet as she noted the Westons' raised eyebrows, Jeff's intrigued look, and Herb's open mouth.

"I don't understand," Delia Weston started to say, when Krista cut into her words.

"Since we work together so much, Ryan has got in the habit of using my maiden name." She flashed him a bright smile which didn't reach her eyes as she turned to the brunette. "Legally, it's Talbot. Mrs. Ryan Talbot." The words came out in distinct icy chips.

Jeff tossed Krista a grin which acknowledged her triumph as he got back into the bus beside her. "Since we're all getting acquainted," he told Ryan blithely, "you won't mind if I start with your wife. There's plenty of room for you and Eve on the seat behind us. We can trade off later."

Ryan opened his mouth to protest and then intercepted the full force of Krista's smoldering gaze. If looks could kill, his body would be laid out flat at her feet. He took a deep breath and wondered how long it would be before he could talk her around. Frowning, he watched Hamid get back into the driver's seat and turn on the ignition.

"Our next stop will be Fez—one of Morocco's old royal cities," the guide announced smoothly. "We should be there in good time for dinner."

"Hallelujah!" Jeff said, looking at his watch. "We're leaving right on time. You'll be glad to see this part of the country in daylight," he told Krista.

Eve glanced across at Ryan's preoccupied profile. "This should be fun, don't you think?"

He caught the tag end of a disdainful look from Krista and then he was given a clear view of the back of her head. Obviously that was all he was going to see of his wife for the next few hours. His eyebrows drew together as he saw Jeff bend attentively over her.

"Don't you think so, Ryan?" There was an exasperated undertone to Eve's question.

"Sorry . . . what was it you said?"

She flounced angrily on the seat, making her thin silver bracelets jingle. "I said that the trip was going to be fun. Now"—she drawled the words out—"I'm not so sure."

Ryan's glance remained stolidly fixed on the back of Krista's head. "I know what you mean, Miss Lenz," he said grimly. "My sentiments exactly."

Chapter *TWO*

If Ryan had only known, his wife was sharing those sentiments as well.

The fact that he had forgotten their married state after his first glimpse of Eve was enough to send Krista's spirits to subterranean level. Even Jeff Snow's flattering attention on the long ride from Tangier south toward the royal city of Fez hadn't really improved her morale. For pride's sake, she had dutifully kept her attention on the road ahead of them and tried to make intelligent responses at the proper time.

She had carefully stared at the peaceful countryside with its stands of eucalyptus and palm trees dotted over the miles of gently rolling grassy slopes. Each time they passed the friendly shepherds standing guard over their flocks of sheep and goats, her hand was raised in response to their greeting, but her heart wasn't in it.

If only Eve Lenz hadn't appeared just then, she argued inwardly. Or when she did appear, why couldn't she have been one of those efficient, hearty creatures instead of looking like a leading lady from the Cannes Film Festival. Of course, that still wasn't any excuse for Ryan's benumbed reaction. Krista's mouth tightened as she stared through the glass at her side. If the female helpers at Woodsea could have seen him then——he would have been without any volunteer guides for the rest of the season. Evidently he wasn't woman-shy, he merely hadn't met anybody as gorgeous as Eve Lenz before. Heaven knew what would happen after a week on the same tour with her.

Krista took a deep breath and straightened her shoulders. She could show him that it worked both ways. At least she could pretend to be engrossed in her surroundings and companion.

"You haven't been listening to a word I've said," Jeff complained at her side. "How are you going to dazzle the folks back home if you don't pay attention to the guide service on this tour? Actually, you'd do better to listen to Hamid, but Herbie and the Westons have him pretty well cornered." He glanced casually over his shoulder. "And from all appearances, Eve is reading her guidebook to your husband." He took another quick look. "He's either asleep or listening with his eyes closed. Which is it?"

Krista sat up straighter, unaccountably cheered by the report. Possibly Ryan wasn't as deeply smitten as he'd appeared. She turned to Jeff and smiled. "Who knows? Did I miss anything important? To be honest, I was starting to count donkeys on the side of the road—but they acted like counting sheep at night."

"So you were sleeping with your eyes open! Thanks a lot. That explains my devastating personality," Jeff said without rancor.

Krista decided to tell him part of the truth. "Chalk some of it up to a lack of sleep last night," she confessed. "They were holding a motor scooter convention for southern Spain under my windows. Very different from this road. . . ." She nodded toward the empty highway ahead of them. "Even the donkeys are quiet here. Did you notice that the men are the only ones who ride them? The women walk alongside."

"Don't blame me," Jeff said hastily. "It's strictly local custom. But from an observer's viewpoint, I think the women have the better part of it. Hanging onto the backbone of a donkey with your legs draped over a bunch of sticks or a loaded basket comes below economy class for my money. Not that I haven't been on a few airplanes where the conditions were remarkably similar," he added.

Krista chuckled. "I wasn't unhappy about that part of our flight this time. The only things that made me uneasy were all the cemeteries the bus passed on the way to the terminal. If I were on the Board of Directors at Kennedy Airport, I'd insist that the drivers take another route." She peered out the window and added, "Speaking of cemeteries"—she pointed toward a Moslem burial place on the left side of the highway—"what on earth are all those people going in that one for? Is it a funeral?"

Hamid overheard her. "No, Mrs. Talbot. This is Friday, a Holy Day in the Moslem religion. Families go to our cemeteries to spend the day with the dead. They put food and water on the graves so that the souls of the departed can share it. After a half hour or so, they collect it again and enjoy their picnic."

"I see," Krista murmured.

"Actually they have other distinctive customs in this country," Delia Weston added with authority. "The dead are always wrapped in white linen and interred in the ground on their sides facing east. Toward Mecca, of course."

"Couldn't we discuss something a little more cheerful?" Eve protested from the back seat. "All this talk about dead bodies seems morbid to me."

"I was merely imparting some information . . ." Delia said stiffly.

"Perhaps you ladies would be interested in the decorations our Moroccan women use," Hamid cut in, as he lowered his speed to pass a family group on the shoulder of the road.

Krista stared back at them. "What decorations? There's hardly any skin showing. They're wrapped in djellabahs and veils from eyebrows to ankles."

"Tomorrow, in the market, look at their hands," Hamid told her. "The backs of them are tattooed with designs."

"Whatever for?" Eve asked.

"To show which tribe they belong to."

"It's hardly an enlightened custom," Delia sniffed.

"Nevertheless, it's an important one. Morocco consists of a tribal society," Hamid reminded her. "All the land we've been driving through since we left Tangier either belongs to the government or to the tribes."

"I've been wondering how they managed without any fences," Ryan put in. "Don't the people have any disputes about boundaries or grazing rights?"

"They're all settled by the headman of the tribe if they do," Hamid explained. "The system functions satisfactorily most of the time."

Eve was peering through the bus window at another group of women walking on the side of the road. "That looks like henna they've put on their hands and feet. Does it serve a purpose like the tattoos or is it strictly decoration?"

"Half and half," Hamid said. "Henna toughens their skin and makes it easier for them to work barefooted in the fields. The Moroccan woman doesn't have an easy life—her life-span is quite limited. I expect you have statistics on that, Mr. Weston," he added politely.

Herb Freeman cut in before the Public Health man could start to expound. "How many wives do they allow in this country?"

Luther Weston wasn't about to be deprived of a chance to impart information. He answered before Hamid could. "Each man can legally have four wives," he droned in precise tones. "The present king has two—a Moroccan woman who is the mother of the Crown Prince and a French wife as well."

"But only a pure Moroccan can inherit the throne," Hamid interjected. "No other bloodline would be acceptable."

"Well, let's get back to the ordinary guys," Herb said. "Do you mean to say that most of these fellows can afford to support four wives?" He rubbed the back of his neck. "They must manage their budgets better than I do."

"Not necessarily. It's a question of practicality," Hamid said. "Men who live in the city generally have two wives—those in the country have four."

"Don't tell me . . . let me guess." There was an acid tone in Delia's voice. "The men need extra hands for labor in the fields. It simply isn't fair."

Hamid seemed amused. "I wouldn't know, Mrs. Weston. I'm not married. You'll have to ask the women."

"They look happy enough," Eve reported. "What about the veils? Do they have to wear them?"

"You'll see more in the country than in a big city like Casablanca. A Moroccan girl can wear a veil at age fifteen if she chooses. Here in the north, the colors mean different things ... like whether she's engaged or married."

"Does the same hold true for the tarboosh or fez?" Ryan asked. "Which is it, by the way?"

"Tarboosh is correct," Hamid assured him over his shoulder. "And the color is significant—if you see a man wearing a red one, he's of Arabic descent; if he wears white, he's a Berber or very religious. Black means he's Jewish, and gray indicates he's a teacher or learned man. If they wear other colors"—Hamid took one hand from the steering wheel to make an expansive gesture—"that means they're Berbers but not religious."

Eve closed her guidebook with a thud. "That's quite enough. My head's swimming with facts already. Would anyone else like a cold drink or coffee or something?"

"It sounds good to me," Herb Freeman said, "and it looks as if there's a settlement up the road. At least the traffic's backing up." He turned to Hamid. "What's happening?"

"Nothing unusual." The other was frowning with concentration as he lessened their speed. "Probably another roadblock. I didn't think there were any on this road. It must have been put up in the middle of the day."

"Roadblocks!" Eve leaned forward to peer through the front windshield. "Whatever for?"

"Evidently you haven't kept up with the political situation over here," Luther Weston said. "Ever since the recent assassination attempts on their King, the government hasn't taken any chances."

Ryan leaned forward as well, resting his arms on the back of Jeff's seat. "But those attempts were a couple years ago. Why all the fuss now?"

"There have been other uprisings," Hamid told

him. "None of them important enough to get in the foreign papers. Just last week, some military figures were arrested at a small town not far from here." He slowed to turn off the main highway at the outskirts of a village. "We might as well have some refreshments before we get in line for the roadblock," he said. "Perhaps by then there won't be so many cars ahead of us. There's a small café nearby which isn't too bad." He drove along a palm-lined street toward the center of a sleepy little town still dozing in the rays of the late afternoon sun. Eventually he pulled up and parked in front of a one-story building with a few iron tables and chairs by the side of it. "This place isn't air-conditioned," he told them apologetically as he turned off the ignition, "but usually there's a breeze. We call it the Sirocco . . . that's a hot wind from the desert. At times it's a mixed blessing."

"When you take a look at the fertile land we've been crossing, it's hard to realize that we're so close to the Sahara," Krista murmured.

Hamid opened his door and smiled. "Sometimes when the Sirocco blows, the Sahara feels as if it's just over the hill."

Delia and Luther struggled out their side of the bus, leaving Herb to trail after them.

Jeff opened his door and held up a hand to assist Krista. "I'll snag a table for the four of us," he told Ryan and Eve, who had assembled on the curb beside him.

"OK, I'll go in with you," Ryan said after a hasty look at Krista's stony profile. "Do you both want cokes?"

"Don't bother with anything for me," Krista announced. The prospect of making small talk with Eve hanging possessively onto Ryan's arm was simply beyond her. "I'll get some exercise while we're stopped. Some of these other shops look interesting."

"Well, *I'm* thirsty." Eve reached across with her other hand and caught Jeff's arm as he hesitated, obviously wondering whether to accompany Krista or not. "Let's see what else they have for sale inside."

"Have fun," Krista told them lightly, determined not to show her annoyance at Eve's casual usurping of all unattached males. "I'll see you later."

She walked quickly along a narrow sidewalk, making way for a veiled woman in a djellabah who was urging a heavily-laden donkey on with a stick. Krista was amused to see that the woman was also carrying a plastic shopping bag and wearing a pair of rubber thongs on her feet under the formal Arabic garb. Evidently the "Made in Japan" label had penetrated North African boundaries as well.

A few feet beyond there was a primitive eating place with a young man cooking lamb kebabs over a charcoal brazier. He grinned at Krista and offered her one of the pieces of meat, saying something in Arabic at the same time.

"*Merci*—no." She shook her head and smiled in return before moving on, happy that Hamid had mentioned French was still taught in Moroccan schools as well as classical Arabic. The only trouble was, her French was almost as nonexistent as her Arabic. If only she'd had time for a crash course before they left home. That made her think of Ryan again and she frowned anew.

Her expression obviously puzzled the Moroccan men who were seated at primitive tables and drinking glasses of mint tea just beyond the shish kebab salesman. Their gaze followed her slim

figure impassively until she realized she'd run out
of local shops and had to turn back the way she'd
come. As she neared the other café and saw the
members of her group, she abruptly decided to
retrieve the orange from her basket and enjoy it
as she walked down to the other end of the
street. At least it would provide an excuse for not
sitting in the empty chair at the metal table
beside Ryan.

She shot him a covert glance and noted that he
was watching her approach with a frown.
Deliberately, she moved over to the far side of the
van before he could hail her.

Hamid made his way to her as she opened the
bus door and started to root around in her basket
for the elusive orange.

"Could I help you find anything, Mrs. Talbot?"

"Thanks, no. . . ." She finally unearthed the
fruit and pulled it out triumphantly. "I thought
I'd eat this while I walked."

He nodded in preoccupied fashion and slammed
the bus door behind her. "There's not much to see
in this town. There's a small shop nearby that
sells many things . . . I think you'd call it a
general store in the States." He fell into step
beside her. "Do you mind if I walk with you?"

"Not at all." She felt almost giddy with success
as they strolled off. Another glance had revealed
Ryan's starting to get up and then subsiding at
his table with a distinctively annoyed look on his
face. "There's nothing oppressive about the
Sirocco today," she said, pushing back her hair
with one hand and enjoying the slight breeze
which stirred the palm fronds over them. "You
can even smell the orange groves at the edge of
town."

"Much more pleasant than many of our smells,"

Hamid agreed as they parted to avoid some animal dung on the edge of the sidewalk. He sighed. "We still have a long way to go in our country before achieving Western progress."

"Don't be in too much of a hurry," she warned. "It's been years since I've seen such a blue sky and fleecy white clouds as you have here. Ecologists will be flocking to Morocco one of these days."

His steps slowed and he stared across at her. "I think you are truly in sympathy with us, Mrs. Talbot. Would you permit me to give you a token gift—a gift of welcome?" He was undoing the buttons at the throat of his djellabah as he spoke. Reaching into a breast pocket, he drew out a thin booklet bound in soft red Moroccan leather and pressed it into her hands.

"Oh, I don't think I should accept anything. . . ."

"Please, Mrs. Talbot." He drew back when she would have returned it to him. "It isn't of any particular value other than as a souvenir of my country. I hope you'll keep it." He watched as she thumbed through the parchment pages covered with Arabic characters.

"It's very lovely." Krista smiled at him uncertainly. "You know, of course, that I can't understand a word of it."

"When you get home again, someone can translate it for you. Actually the contents are just a collection of proverbs and some sayings from the Koran."

"Well, if you're sure . . . I'd be pleased to have it."

"I'm honored, Mrs. Talbot." Then his relieved smile faltered. "You understand, I don't have one for each of the ladies on the tour. . . ."

"So you'd rather I kept quiet about it." Krista

nodded. "Don't worry, I won't say a word. I'll tuck it away in my purse. . . ." She fumbled with the zipper on her shoulder bag and stowed the thin volume in its capacious depths.

"Of course you can tell your husband"—Hamid strove to make his position clear—"but I don't want to hurt the others."

"I understand," she said vaguely as her attention focused on the shop they were approaching. "Good heavens, they *do* sell everything, don't they?" She was staring at hanks of clothesline piled onto displays of dates and spilling over into a tray of red peppers. Bolts of bright cotton fabric were leaning precariously against a stack of crude clay dishes at the end of the counter, and at the front a pyramid of oranges made a dazzling display.

Krista laughed as she looked down at the orange in her hand. "This was really bringing coals to Newcastle, wasn't it? I'll bet Moroccan oranges are better."

Hamid nodded proudly. "As sweet as honey. You'll see tomorrow morning at breakfast." Glancing at his watch, he added, "But we'd better get started again or they won't hold our reservations at the hotel in Fez."

Krista turned obediently to stroll back down the block with him. "Is it difficult to get hotel reservations here?"

"Almost impossible if you don't work months ahead. Our tourist figures go up each year and there simply aren't enough facilities to care for all the visitors. But don't worry; you conference people have all been taken care of."

"Why don't they build more rooms?"

"Tourism comes under a government agency and such things take time . . . much time. However, there's no need for concern, Mrs. Talbot," he reiterated, "I have arranged the very best for your group."

"You mean, our accommodations are all set?" she asked with an uneasy feeling.

"Absolutely. I'm sure you and your husband will be pleased."

"Mmmm. I hope you're right."

As they approached the bus, though, it was evident that Ryan was *not* pleased just then. He was standing by the open door of the vehicle with his arms folded across his chest staring angrily at their approach. Jeff and Eve were still sitting at the table and stood up only as Hamid went around on the driver's side to open the doors over there. Krista would have followed him if Ryan hadn't clamped onto her elbow as she went by.

"Get in," he said in a tone that brooked no argument. "Right now."

"It's easier from the other side. . . ."

"Not when you're sitting on the back seat with me." He put a hand at either side of her waist and boosted her inside the van as he spoke.

"I'm not sitting with you . . ." she protested.

"The hell you're not." He pushed her across to the far side of the back seat and sat down beside her. "Any more shenanigans and I'll have your hide," he added in an undertone as the others approached.

Krista opened her mouth, then took another look at his expression and decided to postpone any ultimatums.

It appeared that both Jeff and Eve were tempted to comment on the new arrangement as they straggled into the bus. Ryan forestalled all objections by hauling out his paperback book on Morocco and burying his nose in it.

"Everybody ready?" Hamid wanted to know.

"All present and accounted for," Luther assured him. "But you'd better tell us what to expect at the roadblock."

"You shouldn't have any problems." Hamid shifted into low and made a sharp left turn to get back on the highway. "The authorities aren't interested in visitors."

"Well, if they're not interested in foreigners, what *are* they interested in?" Eve was peering ahead to try to determine how many vehicles were backed up as they approached the roadblock.

"Illegal shipments of arms among other things. Any evidence of subversive political activity is suspicious." He braked behind a truck piled high with crates of oranges and let the motor idle. "The assassination attempts are responsible for all this. It's apt to go on for months."

Herb was staring through the window on his side. "Boy, they aren't taking any chances on people getting through. There's a regular zigzag pattern to enforce one-lane traffic."

Eve was trying to see, too. "I don't understand. . . ."

"It's simple. If you don't follow the indicated route, you have to drive over those iron spikes on the road. There isn't a tire made that could last three seconds after that. What a setup!"

"And the military trucks pulled up on either side of the road keep people from turning out on the shoulders," Luther put in.

Herb scratched his ear and turned to Hamid, who was observing the whole operation. "I'd hate to try to beat the rap on this. Are you sure that everything's OK? Those fellows standing on the sidelines are carrying machine guns."

"There will be no problems," Hamid said impassively. "Have your passports ready in case they want to see them."

"First I'm searched at the Madrid airport and now this ..." Eve grumbled, as she reached for her purse. "I'll certainly be ready for a cold shower when we finally get to our hotel."

"I'm sorry for the inconvenience, but I know you will be pleased with your accommodation," Hamid assured her. "There's a large swimming pool at the hotel to help you relax."

"Well, that's some consolation," she acknowledged as they inched ahead in the line of traffic. "You didn't have any trouble getting a single room for me, did you?"

"It wasn't easy but I secured the last one available. Mr. Freeman and Mr. Snow will have to share a room as there was such a shortage. Of course, there were no difficulties for the Westons and the Talbots," Hamid was watching the traffic in front of them. "Ah, we're next," he said as the truck full of oranges was allowed to proceed after soldiers had inspected some of the crates. "Don't worry ... this is simply routine." He switched from English to Arabic as the officer in charge approached the van.

Krista scarcely paid any attention to the inspection as her thoughts were still on Hamid's other comment. She did manage to nod and smile when the military official greeted them as he glanced at their luggage piled in the rear of the van. After another lengthy conversation in Arabic, Hamid got out of the driver's seat and accompanied the officer out of their sight behind one of the military vehicles parked at the side of the road.

"Now what?" Eve wanted to know.

"We wait and see, I guess," Jeff told her.

"Nobody looks very upset. It's probably nothing serious."

"There's no need for you to look so alarmed," Ryan said in a low tone close to Krista's ear. "You heard Jeff. These countries are in the throes of a power struggle half the time."

She gave him an exasperated look. "Who's worried about politics, for heaven's sake? Did you hear Hamid when he was telling about the hotel? Eve Lenz has the only single room going."

Ryan's eyebrows came together in a straight line as her murmured complaint registered. Then he shrugged and said, "Maybe she'll agree to having a cot put in if you ask her nicely."

"I can't do that. . . ."

"You mean I'm the lesser of the two evils?" His slanted grin widened at her affronted expression. "That *is* coming up in the world."

"Well, if you think I'm going to ask that Austrian Mata Hari any favors . . ."

"For pete's sake, keep your voice down or she'll hear you." He shot a warning glance to the front of the van, where the rest of the group were huddled in an earnest discussion concerning Hamid's whereabouts.

"She hasn't heard a word I've said ever since we were introduced. Women like that only pay attention to men." As he stirred uneasily beside her, Krista added in a waspish tone, "To think you were giving me a bad time about being 'Miss Blake' with that officer on the *Ibn Batuta* . . ."

"I was afraid you'd get around to that sooner or later," Ryan muttered. "Where in the dickens is Hamid? We'll broil if we sit here much longer."

"Frankly, I think you're just trying to change the subject."

"Damned right I am," he drawled. "At least I

won't make any more mistakes if we keep on this
way."

"What do you mean?"

"Ever since Tangier, I've felt thoroughly married," he told her with some asperity. "You might
try displaying a little wifely affection in front of
the others, at least."

She scowled, but before she could reply, Herb
Freeman announced, "Here comes Hamid now. I
was beginning to wonder if they'd carried him off
to the pokey."

There was a pause while all of them turned to
inspect their guide's appearance as he strolled
toward the bus, settling his djellabah more comfortably about his shoulders.

They waited until he'd slid in the driver's seat
before Eve asked, "Is everything all right? Can we
go now?"

Hamid smiled and took time out to salute the
soldiers standing at the side of the road before
starting the engine. "All clear. The next stop is
Fez."

"No more roadblocks on the way?" Jeff wanted
to know.

"No more delays. I have the captain's word for
it."

"Did they give you a bad time?" Herb asked.

"Now, Mr. Freeman, do I look as if I'd been
handled roughly?" Hamid sounded reproving.
"You must not get the wrong idea of my country.
Newspaper accounts print only sensational news.
The wise man sifts all the evidence before making
up his mind." As he spoke, he was steering the
van in a careful zigzag around the sets of wicked-
looking spikes on the road, then he accelerated as
they left them behind. "Now—only twenty more

miles to the royal city of Fez. The really out-standing part of our trip is about to occur."

"He doesn't know what a prophet he is," Ryan murmured wickedly for Krista's benefit. "Nothing like sharing a room to get to know each other better."

She glared at him. "I may spend the night on a mattress next to the swimming pool."

"Not if you want a job at Woodrea when you get back."

"That's blackmail. . . ."

He thought for a minute and nodded. "So it is—pure and unadulterated."

"But you couldn't ... you wouldn't!" Words failed her.

"Oh, yes, I would. Make no mistake about that." His tone was absolutely definite. "You follow the rules or pay the penalty."

"I never thought you'd play the heavy employer. . . ."

"Then you've learned something new already," he said with some amusement.

Krista flounced away from him on the seat and encountered Hamid's glance in the rear vision mirror.

"Are you enjoying yourself, Mrs. Talbot?" he asked hopefully. "You look as if you're an-ticipating the romance of our country."

Ryan draped his arm purposefully around her shoulders and answered for her. "Mrs. Talbot," he told all of them definitely, "is having the time of her life."

Chapter *THREE*

The sun was just setting as Hamid brought the van into the outskirts of the historic city of Fez.

Krista caught her breath with delight as they drove down the palm-lined boulevards past the old quarter, whose history dated back to the ninth century, and then past newer buildings magnificently decorated with intricate mosaic and thick brass doors on the courtyards.

The last rays of sunlight glinted across the shining green tiles on the roofs of mosques and official buildings, giving them a jewel-like beauty further enhanced by tropical gardens surrounding them. Clusters of bougainvillea and oleander vied with each other on patio walls and bright red and white hibiscus filled the flower beds beneath them.

Hamid noted the group's entranced silence with a pleased smile. "I thought you would like Fez," he announced. "It's said to be the most typical of all Moroccan cities. Tomorrow, we'll take time to explore the medina in the old part of town before we drive on to Marrakesh."

"What's the medina—some kind of souk?" Eve wanted to know.

He shrugged. "Visitors use our terms indiscriminately. A souk is a market . . . the medina is a market . . . although the word medina really means city. Tomorrow you'll see what I mean."

"Then what's a casbah?" Herb asked.

"Despite what your Hollywood moviemakers say, a casbah is a fort," Hamid explained patiently. He lifted a hand from the steering wheel when Eve started to argue with him. "I know, Miss Lenz —all of us have seen Bogart and Boyer epics . . . but we didn't recognize anything."

"That's all right," Ryan told him. "Providing that you don't come out west in the States looking for the cowboys and Indians. We don't recognize anything either."

Hamid's smile broadened. "Then we understand each other." He managed another look at Eve. "Don't worry, Miss Lenz—I think you'll find our medina even more exciting than the Hollywood films. Some of our people never leave it; they're born there, work there, and eventually die there."

"I don't know about the medina but the rest of Fez is magnificent," Krista commented. "It looks like something out of the Arabian Nights." Then, as he pulled into a circular hotel drive, "Good heavens, is this where we're staying?"

Hamid nodded and braked with a flourish before an extravagantly modern two-story stucco building which looked more like Palm Springs than the fabled interior of Morocco.

"Nothing of the Arabian Nights about this place," Ryan said, "unless it's a twentieth century version."

"Give it a chance," Jeff drawled. "Don't forget, twentieth century inventions also include air-conditioning, plumbing that works, and filtered swimming pools."

Ryan grinned and opened the door beside him. "I stand corrected. Lead on, Hamid."

Hamid paused on the wide stone steps. "If

you'll walk through there and wait in the lobby, I'll get your keys for you and arrange for the luggage to be delivered to your rooms."

"What about dinner?" Luther Weston asked as he helped his wife get stiffly down from the bus. "I hope they're still serving this late."

"I shall find out," Hamid promised before disappearing through the lobby doors.

Eve and Jeff waited with Ryan while Krista reached back to drag her basket from the end of the seat.

The Austrian woman looked amused as she emerged with it. Her glance rested on the box of cookies spilling out of the top. "At least you don't have to worry about the dining room being closed, do you, Krista? You might tell Luther that you have a reserve supply."

Her malicious undertone made Krista flush and she tried to hide the basket behind her skirts.

Ryan came unexpectedly to her defense. "Actually," he told Eve, "Krista carries all of our breakables in there. I'm not keen on having our suitcases drenched with shaving lotion and perfume."

Jeff nodded understandingly. "I had some liquid shoe polish spill the last time I was abroad. The stuff never would come out so I had to scratch one perfectly good sport jacket. Nowadays, I go around with suede shoes or scuffed ones"—he held out a foot to demonstrate—"I'm not taking any more chances."

Hamid came back then, carrying a list and a handful of keys. "Mr. Snow . . . you and Mr. Freeman have Room 109; Miss Lenz, 111; Mr. and Mrs. Talbot Room 113. All of these overlook the swimming pool and the inner courtyard so there will be no street noises. Now I'll get a porter for the luggage." He hurried off and vanished in a hallway beyond the reception desk.

"I'm going to take a look at the swimming pool first," Eve announced. "Who's coming with me?"

"I am. I might just spend the rest of the night in there," Jeff said, wiping his forehead with a handkerchief. "How about you, Ryan?"

"Sure ... if there isn't too much chlorine." He turned to Krista. "Does a swim appeal to you?"

She would have agreed enthusiastically if Eve hadn't taken a possessive grip on his arm before she could reply. Ryan merely waited, without attempting to brush her off.

Krista bit down hard on the edge of her lower lip. "I'll see," she said airily and reached over to pluck their room key from his fingers. "I'll go up and check the accommodations first. See you later."

When she traversed the long hallway down one wing of the U-shaped building and finally unlocked their door, the rest of her vague misgivings crystallized into reality.

There was only one large room with twin beds plus an adjoining tiled bath. At the far end of the bedroom, a sliding glass door revealed a small balcony overlooking the inner patio gardens and swimming pool.

Krista's dismayed glance took in the two-foot space between the twin beds occupied by the conventional bed table and reading lamps. The only other furniture in the room consisted of a small round table near the balcony flanked by two little bedroom chairs. If the chairs had been pushed together, only a midget could have managed a possible rest. Not, Krista knew with certainty, a long-legged zoologist with a perfectly legal marriage license on file.

She pushed aside the sliding glass door and stepped out on the balcony, preferring even the warm breeze to the chill of the room's air-conditioning. Her glance moved over the leather screen behind a balcony lounge and then went back to focus on it more carefully. Evidently it provided a measure of privacy for guests who wanted to sunbathe. Her eyes gleamed suddenly with inspiration and she decided there was more than one way to beat the system.

When Ryan pushed open the hall door and set their suitcases inside a few minutes later, he found Krista still breathing hard from settling the leather screen between their two beds. Her satisfied smile faded at his stony expression.

"What's the matter? I thought you'd be pleased," she faltered.

He closed the door behind him and hoisted his case onto the luggage rack in the hall before answering. "Oh, I am." There was no mistaking the sarcasm in his tone. "I'm just surprised you haven't found a piece of chalk to mark a line on the floor by now." He snapped open the locks on his bag with a decisive click. "No wonder you couldn't wait to get up here. What's the matter? Were you afraid that I wouldn't let you move the screen?" He paused in the process of searching through his belongings to give her an enigmatic look. "You needn't have bothered, you know. You were perfectly safe without it." Then, after a suggestive pause, "Or did you think that your bridegroom would get carried away by the tropical Moroccan nights?"

Krista's cheeks flamed at his cutting words. She stood by the end of the screen, nervously clasping her fingers and wondering what had happened to the cool, impassive employer she had known before they had become co-signers on a marriage license. "I wasn't worried," she managed finally. "That wasn't why I did it."

"God, you don't have to tell me that." Ryan yanked his swim trunks from the suitcase and disappeared in the bath just long enough to grab a towel to put around them. "Hamid says dinner will be served for the next hour or so. You can come down when you want—I'll be ready when you are."

His offhand manner brought her pride to the fore. "There's no need for you to bother. Actually I have some letters to write ... maybe I'll just call room service."

His lips settled in an ominous line as he stared at her. "Why don't you do that ... but don't wait up for me," he added over his shoulder at the door. "Some of the bunch want to explore the town. I'll try to be quiet when I come in. Sleep well, Krista." He gave her a scathing parting glance. "You won't be disturbed."

Strangely enough, she wasn't.

After she finally went to bed out of sheer boredom—without writing her letters or bothering with dinner—she fell into a deep sleep of utter exhaustion.

The next sound she heard was something bumping against her mattress. She opened her eyes to find the morning sun streaming in through the open balcony door and Ryan in the process of moving the leather screen back to its normal place outside.

She raised herself on an elbow and blinked in confusion. He was fully dressed in tropical slacks and a dark green knit sport shirt which made his tanned skin look as if he'd spent the last month in the sun. That reminded her of her sunburn and she raised a finger to test the skin on the top of her nose. Midway through the experiment she became aware of the transparency of her gown, which was trimmed at the bodice with attractive but undeniably flimsy eyelet lace. She made a grab for the sheet and pulled it up to her chin as Ryan turned his impassive but sweeping masculine gaze on her.

"What do you think you're doing?" she asked, deciding to take the offensive.

He gave the screen a final push onto the balcony and closed the sliding door behind him as he came back into the bedroom. "I thought I'd remove the evidence before the room service waiter appeared with your breakfast."

"Oh." She tried to achieve a more dignified position without losing her grip on the sheet.

"Here . . ." He bent over his bed and borrowed a pillow to stuff behind her. "I'd suggest you put on some clothes before you answer the door. I'll be back in about a half hour and you're to have your bag ready. Hamid wants to make an early start."

"Where are you going?" Despite her intentions, Krista's tone sounded definitely aggrieved.

Ryan paused by the door. "Down to the dining room to have breakfast. I thought you'd appreciate the extra privacy." His brows drew together as he saw her uncertain expression. "For Lord's sake, get some food into you. Eight hours' sleep doesn't look as if it's done you any good at all." He shoved his hands into his pockets and moved back to the foot of the bed. "What did you have for dinner last night?"

She managed a defiant glance through half-closed lids. "I wasn't hungry." There was no point in adding that she still wasn't hungry and that she felt just as grim as she apparently looked.

A muscle twitched at his jawline. "Look, Krista . . . don't be a damned fool! You have to eat properly when you're traveling. Surely you know enough about nutrition to realize that."

"You needn't lecture me. . . ."

"I'd like to whale the tar out of you—" He gave her a final exasperated glance. "If you don't behave, I'll stick close enough to ensure that you do. *That* should be enough of a threat to make you follow orders."

Krista stared blankly at the hall door for a moment after he'd closed it behind him. Then she swung her feet onto the floor and padded over to her suitcase to hastily don her robe as he'd suggested. By the time the room service waiter had arrived with her Continental breakfast, she'd washed her face and combed her hair into a semblance of order.

She stared distastefully down at the coffee and plate of croissants before breaking off the end of a roll and buttering it. Ryan was quite capable of carrying through his threat and checking to see whether she'd eaten breakfast as he'd ordered.

The roll was absolutely tasteless and the coffee bitter enough to make her shudder but she doggedly plowed on. For a moment, she thought of taking the tray out onto the sunny balcony but a glance at the leather screen standing there made her change her mind.

In the bright morning light, her action of the previous night seemed both foolish and completely unnecessary. Ryan couldn't have been more pointed in his disinterest all along—and his anger now was obviously affronted masculine pride rather than frustrated romance.

Krista took another sip of coffee and grimaced. As if anything like a leather screen would discourage a man ready to petition his rights as a lover. Probably Ryan hadn't bothered to even glance around the end of it when he came in after touring the town with Eve. But if he had spent the night on the tiles, how had he known that she'd had eight hours' sleep? She sighed and put her coffee cup back in the saucer. Probably an educated guess. Nothing more.

By the time she heard a warning knock on the door, she was dressed and applying a final dab of lipstick at the mirror. Ryan came in followed by a grinning bellboy.

"Everything's ready," she told him over her shoulder before he could ask. "I'll bring the basket."

"OK." Ryan helped the boy take their luggage out to the cart in the hall and then came back alone. "You look better," he said, leaning against the end of the dressing table as she stowed her lipstick in her bag. "I'm glad you decided to be sensible and eat something."

Krista started to challenge him but her glance wavered before his sardonic one. "I thought you might check up on me," she acknowledged finally, "since you've apparently decided I need a keeper."

"Now you're getting the drift. I know the bill of fare wasn't great but the rolls weren't bad. At least they should keep you going until the morning coffee break."

She shook her head. "Don't mention coffee. I've decided to switch to tea for the duration of the tour. That stuff at breakfast was awful."

"No argument there. Maybe that's why the natives drink mint tea." Ryan bent down and picked up her basket.

"You don't have to carry that ..." she protested.

"I don't mind. Actually"—he rubbed the back of his neck with his free hand and looked embarrassed—"I shoved a couple of my things into it. Breakables ... if you don't mind," he added hesitantly.

Krista smiled for the first time that morning. "No, I don't mind at all." Her eyes were dancing. "Be my guest."

"Thanks. I accept with pleasure."

He held open the door with a flourish. "On to the medina, Mrs. Talbot."

As she started to brush by him in the narrow hall, Krista was aware of every inch of his masculinity. Almost without meaning to, she stopped as she drew level with his chin.

"Ryan—I'm sorry." Her soft words spilled out impulsively. "I was an awful fool last night. Forgive me, please."

For a moment he didn't answer. Then she saw his broad chest move with silent laughter. "My dear Krista ... damned if you're not more trouble than a cage of Bengal tigers. But a hell of a lot more interesting," he added unexpectedly. He drew his finger slowly and deliberately down the soft skin on the inside of her forearm. "Now—make something dastardly of that if you want to."

Krista had to clear her throat before she could manage more than a tremulous response. "Believe it or not, Dr. Talbot," she said distinctly, "this time I don't intend to."

The visit to the crowded serpentine of market stalls in the old medina of Fez was a novel experience, with appeal for all of them. The fact that so many thousand people could live and work in the rabbit warren of shops was unbelievable in itself. The covered walks which protected the shopkeepers from the sun kept them in a gloomy atmosphere that reeked of sinister depths after the bright daylight outside the medina.

Krista found herself elbowed by the natives jamming the narrow walkway. There were old men crouched in doorways, their faces almost hidden by the hoods of their djellabahs. Barefooted youngsters wearing shorts and ragged T-shirts darted through the crowds in an elaborate game of hide-and-seek, irritating the shoppers and earning scornful glances from their older sisters who were carrying unleavened bread loaves to the communal ovens. When the veiled women shoppers stopped to make their purchases in front of the open stores. there were traffic jams beyond belief. Krista wrinkled her nose as the odors of unwashed humanity mingled with the fragrances of the market stalls, thinking it was provident that travel posters lacked this ingredient.

Hamid had warned all of the group to watch their valuables and to try to stay together. This warning lasted only until they had to scatter as a man came driving a laden donkey down the aisle shouting *"Balek"* or "Make way there." Since it was a case of either "make way" or be run down, Arabs and visitors alike hastily flattened themselves against the sides of the stone corridor.

Krista clutched at Ryan's shirt and he put a protective arm around her shoulders, pushing her into the safety of a cubbyhole filled with brooms of all sizes.

"Sorry." He reached down to retrieve her brimmed straw hat from where it had fallen in the midst of a pile of brushes. "I didn't hurt you, did I?"

"Nuh-uh." She pushed the hat back on her head and then stared out into the stream of humanity which had quickly regrouped behind the donkey and now was surging about its business. "Good heavens, did you ever see so many people?"

He rubbed the back of his hand over his forehead. "Quite a thrash. Reminds me of that time last month when I made the mistake of getting between the hippo and the side of his pen." He glanced around to see an Arab shopkeeper sitting cross-legged at the back of the cubicle surveying them dispassionately.

"Maybe we'd better buy something," Krista suggested after noting that their precipitous entry had caused havoc in the shop's main display. No wonder the shopkeeper was giving them the cold and stony.

"I think you're right." Ryan reached down and selected a rattan whisk broom about a foot long. "How about this? It's the smallest thing he's got."

Krista giggled. "Just what I've always wanted. It's going to look great sticking out of the basket."

"Mmmm. It may not get that far." Ryan reached into his pocket and pulled out a handful of coins.

"You're supposed to bargain for everything," she reminded him. "Hamid said so."

"How the devil do you bargain in two different languages?" Ryan countered, giving the shopkeeper another glance. "Besides, this has to cover breaking and entering as well." He selected another coin—a larger one this time—and walked to the back of the shop.

Krista was still clutching the whisk broom when he came back. "What did he say?"

"Absolutely nothing unless a dirty look counts

for anything. Anyhow, he took the money." Ryan caught her elbow. "Come on, let's get out of here."

"I'm with you." Krista's nose twitched. "That butcher shop next door is getting to me."

"It wouldn't be so bad without the flies," Ryan said as they pushed their way into the main corridor again. As they went past he gave the lamb and goat carcasses hanging nearby a perfunctory appraisal. "The prices are great—but a display case and some refrigeration would help. Not that it seems to bother anybody."

They sauntered on for a few minutes until they came to a stop in front of a shop where a man sitting at an old-fashioned treadle sewing machine was sewing djellabahs in the gloom.

Ryan looked up and down the corridor before he muttered, "Where in the dickens is that Nejjarine fountain? Hamid told us to meet there and we're late now."

Krista stood on tiptoe to try to peer through the crowds. "It should be close by—there are supposed to be woodcarvers working in cedar and thuja in that part of the market. It would be nice to have a carved souvenir," she added wistfully.

Ryan grinned. "How about ordering a box for our whisk broom?" He urged her forward. "C'mon, there's a mosque down there to the right ... let's give that direction a try. Hamid said something about a mosque and an abandoned Koran school being close to the fountain."

Krista was trying to keep up with his long steps. "How can you tell there's a mosque?"

He gestured ahead of them. "That tower up there. The one with the white flag on it."

"What does the flag have to do with it?"

"I forgot you weren't along last night when

Hamid was explaining. He said that so many of the people in the medina are illiterate that the priests hoist a flag so everyone will know when it's a holy day."

"Oh." Krista moved along beside him for a minute or two digesting the information. Then, "I didn't know Hamid went along with you last night."

"He was the only one who knew where he was going. Actually you missed a treat. . . ."

"In what way?"

"Hamid shed his djellabah for the latest thing in men's apparel . . . a pale pink bodyshirt and matching flare pants. Even Eve took a second look."

"I can well believe it." Krista's voice was dry. "Were there just the three of you?"

"No—Jeff was along as well. Herb and the Westons begged off after dinner." Ryan peered into a shaded alleyway that led off the main corridor and then pulled her to a halt. "Wait a minute . . . here's something you should see."

Krista obediently followed him into a tiny inner patio where four or five vendors were sitting on their heels beside trays full of a substance that looked like bulk tea. A display of oddly-shaped rocks was piled to one side. She smiled. "All right—I give up. Is it a spice shop?"

Ryan grinned in response. "Nope. Believe it or not, it's the Arab equivalent of a cosmetics shop."

"You're fooling." She bent down to finger one of the piles of green leaves and nodded a greeting to the amiable vendor sitting beside it. "Do you sniff it, eat it . . . or rub it on?" she asked Ryan. "It looks like an herbal tea to me."

"You'd never make it in the harem. That, my dear Krista"—he indicated the greenery—"is henna.

Good for everything from gray hair to tender arches."

"I'll be darned. What are the rocks for?"

"Hamid told us the Arab women use them for scrubbing their hair. Some sort of a shampoo aid."

Krista moved over to weigh one in her hand. "Talk about going back to nature," she marveled, "this is really organic." Her glance lingered on a shelf full of wooden bottles which looked like nail polish containers. "At least I know what those are. It's kohl, isn't it? For making designs on their bodies?"

"Go to the head of the class. Too bad you don't live here. I wouldn't have to worry about any staggering bills from the beauty shop," he said lightly.

"Maybe the women make up for it in other ways. Some of those djellabahs look pretty expensive. And what about those gorgeous sheer caftans in the shop next to the hotel?"

He took the shampoo rock from her hands and replaced it on the tray. "I should have known that you wouldn't have missed any of those."

She followed him out of the courtyard, still laughing. "I thought you'd have picked out a djellabah for yourself by now. Something to wear around the house on weekends when you're smoking your bubble pipe." She indicated an Arab gentleman hurrying past them. "Don't forget to buy a pair of those lovely pointed-toed slippers to go with them."

Ryan's eyes narrowed with amusement at her teasing. "I'll buy my outfit the same time you choose your harem costume. Maybe you can get some ideas at Marrakesh. Hamid said we'll take in a performance of the best belly dancer in the country there."

Krista dodged around two men carrying bottles of water on their shoulders who were shooing three toddlers in front of them. She waited until they were safely past before she looked at Ryan with assumed reproach. "And I thought this was a cultural and scientific tour."

"It is. You can't fault native dances," he replied with a straight face. "I understand the use of the abdominal muscles in a dance of that kind is pure science."

She attempted a severe look but her lips twitched. "I'll wait and see. You know, it would have been fun to have one of those shampoo rocks. . . ." She drew to a halt. "I could go back. . . ."

"No way." He clamped a hand on her shoulder. "This darned whisk broom is bad enough to carry without dragging rocks along as well. They're strictly off limits, along with bird cages. We still have two and a half more weeks in Europe to get through." He broke off to say, "There's Hamid beckoning to us from the courtyard. This must be the college of Bou Inania. How about that for dead reckoning?"

"It's certainly a beautiful place." Krista was staring wide-eyed at the marble and onyx paving surrounding the fabled mosaic fountain where, even then, two men were washing their hands and feet before entering a nearby mosque.

Hamid waved again from a corner stairway. Krista noticed that Eve was watching Jeff take a picture in one of the carved cedar archways; the Westons and Herb were observing a young woodcarver at work.

"Please come here, Mr. and Mrs. Talbot—" There was a ring of impatience in Hamid's voice. "This stairway leads to the roof of the *mdrarsa*

. . . or college. From there, you will enjoy a view over the entire medina. Now be careful going up the stairway—" he cautioned Ryan and Krista as they came up to him. "There are just a few candles for illumination until you come out on the roof."

Krista hadn't gone up more than eight steps before she discovered his warning was the understatement of the year. "Good Lord, I can't see a thing," she muttered to Ryan, who was supposedly behind her. "Can you?"

There was a thud, then his exasperated, "Damn it all! Krista—where are you?"

"Here." She waited until his hand fumbled onto her wrist. "That's me," she said in some confusion. "Is that you?"

"I guess so. Inhale a little so I can get by you— then I'll lead the way. My God, this place is like Gehenna."

She felt his body brush past and then he pulled her along behind him slowly up the stairs. After they had wound upward for another three or four minutes, they came upon a candle stub whose tiny flame flickered in the draft.

Krista stopped to rest, peering back down the winding stair in the murky half-light. "It sounds as if the rest of them are coming up behind us. Isn't that Eve's voice?"

"I guess so. Let's move along. It can't be much farther to the top. I hope the view is worth all this trouble."

When they finally reached the flat roof of the college, even Ryan let out a soft whistle of approval. "It's tremendous, isn't it?" he said to Krista as they made their way to the edge of the roof and peered over into the magnificent courtyard of the nearby mosque. "Look at that tile mosaic on the walls! And those doors! That's the old art of polychrome decoration on wood. In past times, they applied pure gold with 'ox glue' or raw egg whites."

"It's too bad we can't visit any of the mosques and see the inside decorations," Luther Weston was complaining to Hamid as the rest of the group straggled over to them.

Hamid held out his hands helplessly. "This is the law of the country. No foreigners in the mosques. I'm sorry if it inconveniences you."

"Well, it's a good thing we saw some in Turkey," Luther groused. "At least it gives us a basis for comparison."

"It's interesting how they use the cedar beams," Jeff said, joining them. "The carving on the wooden doors blends well with the marble and tile, too." He turned and smiled at Krista. "You're very quiet."

"Probably because I'm overwhelmed," she admitted.

"Actually it reminds me of some of the things in southern Spain," Eve interjected. "The Alhambra reflects the same architecture."

Jeff ignored the interruption. "What part do you like best, Krista?"

He sounded as if he really wanted to know, Krista decided. She surveyed the scene in front of her before replying. "The contrasts, I think. It's so quiet in the courtyard that you can hear the droplets of water falling in the fountain—or the birds fluttering their wings when they land on those gorgeous green tile roofs. Just like a tiny pocket of Paradise—yet just a stone's throw away all those people are surging through the medina."

Hamid nodded understandingly. "And the medina is a cross section of life. As I said before, most of the inhabitants never leave it ... they sleep and eat in a room over their shops—their children are born there and they expect to die there. At least they can take a few minutes off and come in here to refresh their souls."

"Doesn't sound like much of a life to me," Delia Weston said, moving still nearer the railing. "Are they satisfied with that?"

"Are any of us?" Hamid asked. Then, with a shrug, "They are fatalists, Mrs. Weston. *Inn Sha Allah*, they'd say."

"God willing," Ryan murmured.

"Well, it's too hot for me to stand up here and listen to a philosophic discussion." Eve was brushing at a fly droning around her nose. "I'll wait for you all downstairs in the courtyard—in the shade." She strode away toward the head of the stairs.

"Miss Lenz is right," Hamid said, pulling back the sleeve of his djellabah to look at his watch. "About five more minutes, then we should meet down in the courtyard and return to the bus. We still have a long drive to Marrakesh."

"That just gives me time for an overall picture from up here," Jeff said, unzipping his camera case. "What do you think about the light, Ryan?"

Krista watched the two men huddle over their cameras and smiled with amusement. Camera widows ranked along with golf widows, she was finding out. Once a photographer was intent on getting a picture, buildings could topple or the earth could come to an abrupt stop and it wouldn't be noticed until he'd clicked the shutter.

She glanced around the rooftop wishing she could find a patch of shade ... her sunburned nose and forehead were making themselves felt in the blazing African day. After shading her eyes, she decided she'd better follow Eve's example before her complexion crisped at the edges.

She parted her lips to call to Ryan and then decided not to interrupt the photographic session. Once he discovered she was missing, he'd obviously presume that she was waiting below.

Moving over to the entrance of the stairs, she started down, keeping a hand on the curving stone wall. If it had seemed dark on the ascent, it was doubly so now after her sight was weakened by the glaring sunlight. For a moment, she thought of simply sitting down on one of the crudely-cut steps until her vision improved. Then, feeling impatient at her timidity, she fumbled on down the winding stair.

By the time she passed the first candle, she was able to move more rapidly, although it was so dark that the walls were barely apparent in the gloom. She grimaced with exasperation and then cocked her head to listen. Fortunately, there was nothing wrong with her hearing. If anything, it was made more acute by the strangeness of her surroundings and her heightened tension. She had been aware of the sound her shoes made as they felt their way to the edge of each step ... the gritty rasping of her soles on the dusty stone floor.

Now, the sudden quiet seemed oppressive and threatening. She started down the stairs again, hoping that if she moved faster she could escape her fear in the daylight at the bottom.

There was an abrupt flurry of movement beside her and she teetered on the edge of the step—trying to regain her balance. She instinctively put out her hands to brace herself even as she felt a heavy blow on her shoulder as someone pushed roughly past. Her scream slashed through the dank air while she grabbed hopelessly for something ... anything ... to halt her headlong plunge.

The echo of that scream was still reverberating when she lost consciousness. Seconds later, the guttering candle on the stair landing below her limp, sprawled figure was snubbed out as well.

Chapter FOUR

It was the sound of voices which brought her back to consciousness.

Ryan's first. His deep tones sounded strangely rough and uneven close by her ear. "Krista honey . . . are you all right? Can you hear me?

Then Jeff's. "I think she's coming 'round. You'd better give her more room."

Eve's sounded far-off. "I don't see why there's all this fuss when a woman faints. Really, it's so stuffy in here I feel dizzy myself."

"Krista doesn't faint." Ryan's sharp reply cut into her complaint. "She must have lost her footing. Otherwise, why would she have screamed? Krista . . . darling." His voice moved closer again. "Can you open your eyes . . . please. . . ."

After that appeal, she decided she'd better try.

It was a distinct effort to pry up her leaden eyelids but she managed. She blinked and turned her head as she found herself staring into a lantern which Hamid was holding over her. "It's so bright," she complained, putting up her hand to shade the glare.

Ryan's grip on her arms tightened so abruptly that she winced. "Oh, God, I'm sorry." He released her immediately, and sat down on the step beside her. "I think I've aged ten years. What happened? No—don't move . . ." he ordered as she started to sit up. "Not until we find out if anything's broken."

"My back will be if I stay here. The edge of the step is boring into it and I must be sitting on my purse." She shifted her hips onto another step.

"Damn it all!" Ryan said savagely through clenched teeth. "Stay put, will you!"

His outburst and the uneven timbre of his voice made her stare at him as he crouched beside her. She hadn't seen him so concerned since a newborn rhino calf fell into the moat last winter. Surely he wasn't this upset over the fact that she'd scraped some skin falling downstairs. For a minute she was tempted to mention the unknown person who had brushed past and made her lose her balance. Then her thoughts were interrupted by Hamid leaning forward anxiously.

"Your husband is right about changing position," he said. "You could be badly injured."

"Well, I'm not." Dimly she noted the other members of the group staring at her from their places on the stairs. Evidently Eve had come up from the courtyard at the sound of trouble, and the others were frowning down at her from the steps above. Krista felt like an exhibit in a display case under their concentrated gaze.

She decided to try her luck on her feet and pushed herself upright before Ryan could stop her. "No . . . don't say anything," she told him, wincing as she tried to put some weight on her right foot. "I'm not hurt except for my ankle. I must have turned it on the steps."

"You're sure?" Ryan asked.

"Positively." She managed a game smile. "How about my nylons?"

He shook his head. "Just a memory. Your knees

don't look too good, either. The sooner you're out of here . . . the better."

Krista nodded, too tired to argue any longer. She looked at Hamid. "Is there somewhere I could clean up?"

"Of course. We'll go to the emergency aid clinic near the center of town. But can you manage the rest of the stairway?" His expression was doubtful.

"I can hobble perfectly well if you'll let me hang onto you," Krista said to Ryan.

"If this damned place weren't so narrow, I'd carry you." He glanced up and down the winding steps with exasperation. "But if I tried, I'd probably send both of us rolling to the bottom."

"Once we're down, we can make a chair and get her to the bus easily," Jeff offered.

"I wish you'd stop talking about me as if I weren't here," Krista complained.

"You're here, all right," Ryan said, putting a firm arm around her waist and pulling her tight against him. "Now hop on your good foot and brace your hand on the wall for support. We'll be down before you know it. Hamid, you lead the way with the lantern."

"Of course," that individual replied.

"I'll be glad to carry your handbag," Delia offered as Krista took the first step.

"Thanks, but I can keep the strap on my shoulder," Krista told her. "I'm such a well-trained tourist by now it's a wonder I don't take it to bed with me."

Delia laughed in sympathy, following them down the stairs. "I know what you mean—the thought of losing my traveler's checks and passport would give me an instant nervous breakdown."

"Wait until you go across Europe on the train," Luther told Krista. "The sleeping car porter takes your tickets and your passport. Delia didn't sleep a wink the first time it happened to us . . . she was afraid he'd forget to return them and we'd be stranded."

"Surely I wasn't as bad as that . . ." Delia countered.

"That's what you say now." Krista saw him give his wife an affectionate hug even as he teased her. "But I have an excellent memory."

"Imagination, I'd say," Delia said tartly. She sighed with relief as they reached the last few steps and the sunlight poured in from the courtyard. "Thank goodness. I think we've all had enough of the Attarine *mdrarsa*."

"Oh, yes!" Krista took a deep breath, wishing she could forget the terror on those dark steps. Now that she was safely out of trouble with Ryan's lean strength beside her, her suspicions that someone had deliberately pushed her seemed incongruous. Certainly too farfetched to mention in front of the others.

"Now, if you'll follow me, there's a shortcut we can take to the bus," Hamid said, handing the lantern to an old caretaker in a stained djellabah who crouched by the steps. The driver didn't bother to speak to him but merely flipped a coin at his feet.

"Put your arms around my neck," Ryan told Krista. She obeyed gingerly and felt him sweep her up in a firm embrace. "OK, let's go," he told Hamid.

"I'm too heavy for you," she started to protest until Ryan's impatient snort cut her off in midsentence.

"I thought I could help on the airlift," Jeff complained mildly as they threaded their way through the shoppers in a main corridor of the medina.

"You're helping by carrying my camera," Ryan said. "Krista's no problem."

The other's determined expression made Jeff simply nod and stride ahead so that he could clear the crowds from their path.

"He should shout *'Balek . . . Balek . . .'* the way they do when the donkeys go through," Krista said with a nervous chuckle. She was trying to keep her shoulder away from Ryan's chest so that he wouldn't think she was taking advantage of his kindness.

If he were reading her mind, he got the wrong translation because his arms tightened and he pulled her against him firmly. "Relax, will you!" His voice was tinged with amusement. "This comes under the heading of first aid . . . nothing more. You don't have to worry about propriety."

"How disappointing." She tried to keep her voice light. "What a comedown after reading about the sheiks tossing women over their shoulders and rushing out to the desert."

Jeff caught the last of her comment and turned to grin at them. "Don't blame Ryan. A man needs a good horse for that maneuver and a deserted tent beside an oasis. A donkey in the medina's not much of a substitute." He nodded ahead of them as Hamid drew up beside their bus and started unlocking doors. "And a mini-bus isn't any better." He went on as the group started to file in. "Hamid, I was telling Mrs. Talbot that we're missing the romance in this country. You're going to have to invent something to please the ladies."

The guide smiled good-naturedly as he came to assist Krista into the vehicle. "There's plenty of

romance left ... you just have to look in the
right places. Actually we drive right by one this
afternoon on the way to Marrakesh. I'll show you
—if Mrs. Talbot feels like it, of course."

"I'll be fine," Krista said, relieved to finally rest
her foot on the car seat. "We can be on our way
after a quick stop at the first aid station."

"You and I will be on our way only after a doctor says you're all right," Ryan told her firmly.
"Not before. Make no mistake about that."

A warm feeling that had nothing to do with
the Moroccan temperature spread over her as his
words sank in. It was nice that he was taking his
... responsibilities ... so seriously. Her mind
sought for the proper word. Or should it be du-
ties? She darted a look at his stern profile as he
dropped onto the seat beside her. It was hard to
tell from his expression whether cosseting a
temporary wife was a burden or not.

He turned to meet her tremulous glance and
she lowered her eyes hastily. At least, she told
herself as Hamid pulled away from the gate of the
medina, if Ryan were suffering, he was certainly
hiding it well.

Fortunately, the doctor who was on duty at
the clinic in the center of town saw no reason why
Krista couldn't accompany the rest to Marrakesh
if she wanted to. After strapping her ankle and
cautioning her to stay off it as much as possible for
the next day or so, he then supervised a middle-
aged nurse who carefully cleansed Krista's scraped
knees and elbows and anointed them with an an-
tibiotic ointment to avoid possible infection.
Finally the doctor prescribed a combination pain-
killer and tranquilizer to make the afternoon's
trip more comfortable. "It's a long ride to Marrakesh," he said in heavily-accented English. "In

another hour ... perhaps two or three, you will discover a new set of muscular bruises. Take two more of these tablets at bedtime for pain. I'll write down the name of a colleague in Marrakesh if you need professional attention." He found a prescription blank and dashed off a line of Arabic on it together with a telephone number and then came over to help Krista down from the metal examination table.

She took the paper and the foil-wrapped tablets. "Thank you, Doctor. You've been very kind."

"Don't be surprised if you do not feel as well later on," he cautioned. "Delayed shock is always unpleasant but this medicine should help. By tomorrow, you'll be much better. Now, I'll tell your husband ... he looked anxious."

"I'm glad I don't have to spoil his holiday." Krista smiled her thanks at the nurse and followed the doctor out to the waiting room where Hamid and Ryan stood by the door. "Practically as good as new," she assured them.

Ryan's face creased in a grin. "Good. Then I won't have to trade you in for a new model."

Hamid nodded approvingly as well and smiled at Ryan's flip comment. "I'm very pleased we can detour around Imichil on our drive this afternoon," he said obscurely.

The guide didn't explain his remark until considerably later in the day when he brought up the subject of new models again. They were halfway between Fez and Marrakesh before he gestured toward a sign marking a side road to the left.

"If you had wanted to trade in Mrs. Talbot," he told Ryan over his shoulder, "we're not far from the place you'd do it. That's the road to Imichil, where they have the Moroccan marriage market."

Not only Krista straightened in her seat at his pronouncement but Delia and Eve as well.

The latter looked up the winding road leading to the towering High Atlas Mountains on their left. "You must be joking," she said in her faintly accented voice. "Surely that sort of thing doesn't go on any longer. Selling women like slaves, I mean."

"Slavery has nothing to do with it, Miss Lenz." Hamid couldn't hide his anger. "You leap to the wrong conclusions. Imichil is a tribal area where our people merely cling to their ancient customs."

"Let him get on with the story, Eve," Jeff interrupted. "If everyone can shop at their market, we might make a detour on the way to Marrakesh. What's another hour or two, eh, Herb?"

"Don't get me involved in this. I can't afford the wife I have," Freeman told him with a rare grin. "But I wouldn't mind looking on, though. Strictly as a spectator."

"Sorry, gentlemen, you're three months too early. The wedding festival or 'Moussem of the Fiancés' isn't held until the end of September." Hamid's tanned features wrinkled with amusement at their crestfallen faces. "You'll have to make another trip."

"You said wedding festival." Delia leaned forward in her seat. "What's so unusual about that?"

"Merely that the Imichil men only have to keep their brides for a year. If they're displeased with them after that time ... they can trade them back at the wedding festival the next year. But not before then," Hamid said virtuously. Then, after her look of disapproval, he added, "You must realize that this part of the country is very isolated and the old customs linger. Imichil itself is located almost seven thousand feet up in the mountains at the edge of the Sahara."

Krista heard a subdued chuckle from Ryan's end of the seat but she kept her gaze straight ahead. "Don't the women object to this high-handed treatment?" she asked Hamid.

"Apparently not, Mrs. Talbot ... it's been going on for centuries. Not only that, it's an occasion for great festivity each year. The women wear their finest silver jewelry and striped robes."

"Maybe they're as pleased to get rid of their husbands as the other way around," Jeff said. "I'll bet there's a great deal of soul-searching about two weeks before the event." He turned and grinned at Eve. "Think of the possibilities."

"A typical male chauvinist reaction," was her only comment. Then her eyes narrowed. "On the other hand, it would be interesting to see what kind of offers a woman could get. Some of the Moroccan mountain tribesmen are extraordinarily good-looking."

"I'm surprised to hear an educated woman like you talking like that," Delia snapped.

Eve smoothed the V-collar of her snug-fitting blouse. "I still say it would be interesting. How do you suppose I'd fare, Hamid?" Her tone was complacent.

"To be truthful, Miss Lenz ... not too well. Arabs like their wives on the plump side. They give seven camels for a fat wife, and five camels for a thin one. That's very different from male thinking in the Western world," he added hastily.

Krista took pity on him in the thick silence that followed. "If I remember, some of those Arab proverbs don't phrase it as diplomatically. Are there any sayings on marriage in that book you gave me?"

"Not that I remember," he replied evasively.

"How about a Portuguese one," Luther contributed. "A goose, a woman, and a goat are bad things lean."

"I don't know any proverbs," Jeff said, "but there was a limerick I remember. Don't worry," he added as Ryan raised an eyebrow, "it's clean."

"Must be different from the limericks I've heard," Herb murmured.

Jeff pressed on:

"There was a young lady of Lynn
Who was so excessively thin
That when she essayed
To drink lemonade
She looked down the straw and fell in."

A gust of laughter followed the last line with even Eve and Delia enjoying it. They were still chuckling when Luther interrupted plaintively.

"I hate to change the subject, but are there any cold drinks left? According to my calculations, it's going to be way past dinner when we get to Marrakesh."

"There should be enough bottles to go around." Ryan turned in the seat and reached down in the luggage well where they were stored. "Hope you don't mind if they're warm," he said handing them forward.

Krista was rooting through her basket. "I have some cookies to help tide you over. They came from a shop in Madrid."

Luther reached back to take the package and pass it around the front of the van. "All handouts gratefully received," he told her thankfully as he took a fistful. "If we hadn't had to wait so long at that last roadblock, we would have arrived at a civilized hour." His glance rested curiously on Hamid. "Is something going on in this area that we don't know about? I shouldn't think government men would be planting roadblocks and stopping traffic on all the main highways unless they're afraid something drastic will happen."

"There *was* a small disturbance with some army cadets in the north last night," Hamid admitted. "I was just informed at the tourist office this morning."

Delia Weston hastily removed the soft drink bottle from her lips. "Well, it's a little late to be telling us now. Luther and I didn't come here to be involved in any political uprisings."

"There's no need to be alarmed, Mrs. Weston," Hamid said. "If my superiors thought there was the slightest danger, all foreigners would be immediately escorted from the country. After all, the only damage sustained so far on this tour," he added lightly, "happened to Mrs. Talbot. And I'm sure she wouldn't blame that on revolutionary activity. Am I right?" His eyes met Krista's in the driving mirror.

She stared back at him, feeling almost impaled by the directness of that dark glance. Her first impulse was to say that someone had been responsible for her plunge down the steps. But a revolutionist ... hardly. She shook her head slightly as if to clear it.

Ryan was frowning at her. "What's the matter, Kris? Aren't you feeling well? Maybe you need something to drink. . . ."

"No, thanks." She managed an apologetic smile. "I'm fine. Just a little groggy from those pills the doctor gave me." She turned back to face the others. "I wish I could blame my clumsiness on the politicians," she said in a light tone, "but that really would be reaching for a scapegoat. It was strictly my fault." She crossed her fingers in her lap as she spoke and it wasn't until a minute or so later that she noticed Ryan's brooding gaze was fixed on them.

Darkness had fallen when Hamid finally drove into the outskirts of Marrakesh, the most romantic city of southern Morocco. Colored spotlights illuminated the Koutoubia minaret and the blooms of the jacaranda trees surrounding it provided a lacy blue frame for the fabled landmark.

"Tomorrow you can see the rest of the city's sights," Hamid told his weary passengers, "but remember to get started early. At this season the heat is often over one hundred and twenty degrees in the middle of the day."

Eve groaned. "What a time to go touring schools."

"Well, it's only for half a day," Jeff reassured her, "and practical research is the reason for this tour." He turned in the seat and looked at Ryan. "You and Krista are scheduled to inspect the Toubkal zoo, aren't you?"

"That's right. We'll have to see how Krista feels in the morning, though."

"You can't leave me in the hotel," she protested. "This is the thing I've been looking forward to."

Eve raised her eyebrows. "Such enthusiasm! I could understand if it was for the souk. That's world-famous. But a private zoo?"

"You're not a zoologist," Jeff said briskly. He bent over his notebook and tried to read it.

"Herb . . . you and Luther are scheduled for a discussion with some of their Public Clinic people."

"That's right," Luther cut in. "Hamid is to drive us and Delia said she'll go along to take notes."

"Then everything is neatly arranged," Jeff said, settling back.

"Not exactly," Eve said. "Just exactly what are *you* going to do?"

He grinned at her. "Not a thing . . . officially. My work's over when all of you are taken care of. I'll stake out a lounge for you at the swimming pool . . . and if you're *very* cooperative, I'll carry your parcels when we visit the souk later in the day. How's that?"

Eve opened her mouth to complain further and then shrugged. "I'm too tired to argue with you. The way I feel now, all I want to do is fall into bed."

"I'm sorry it's been such a long day," Hamid said as he drove past high-walled enclosures which were interspersed with grassy vacant lots at the edge of the city. "Your hotel is just down the way here. It's not the one where Sir Winston Churchill stayed on his vacations but it's very new and luxurious. What's more . . . the air-conditioning works," he added. "That's the really important thing in Marrakesh."

When they finally reached their room after walking along the stifling hotel corridors, both Ryan and Krista were inclined to agree with him. The bedroom almost duplicated their room in Fez with twin beds and a glassed-in balcony at the far end of the room. This time, Krista didn't even bother to see if there were any leather screens around, she merely sank onto the edge of the closest bed as Ryan attended to their luggage and sent the bellboy on his way. Afterward, he took one look at her pale face and opened her suitcase to pull out her gown and robe.

"Put these on," he instructed. "I'll turn down your bed. Can you manage by yourself?" he asked as she stood up wearily and reached for her night things.

"Just about," she admitted, wondering if she'd shatter completely when she tried to walk again. Her throbbing muscles certainly felt like it.

Later, a knock came on the bathroom door while she was still washing her face. Krista frowned and opened the door a crack, trying to keep the suspicion from her voice. "What is it?"

"Not what you evidently suspected," Ryan said with amusement. He thrust a quart bottle of mineral water through the crack. "Here. Stay on the safe side and use this for brushing your teeth."

"Oh, thanks very much. I won't be a minute." She knew that she looked as sheepish as she sounded. So much for her suspicions about Ryan's ulterior motives.

When she came out wearing her pale blue satin robe and carrying her clothes, she noticed he was still fully dressed, although he'd started his own unpacking. "The water didn't taste very good," she said, trying for a casual note as she dumped her lingerie in the suitcase and hunted in the closet for a hanger, "but it was a great improvement over a dry toothbrush."

Ryan calmly came over and hung up her dress before taking her shoulders and steering her toward the bed. "You should try brushing your teeth in orange soda pop the way I did once in Mexico. It's not the greatest, either."

"I can see dentists shuddering all over the

country," she joked while wondering if he actually planned to tuck her in.

Ryan was tact personified on that score. "You get under the covers and I'll bring a glass of water so you can take your medicine."

"I don't think I'll need it," she said, unfastening her watch and putting it on the bed table.

He glanced back from the bathroom door. "Now, look ... I don't mind your arguing with me but don't try to second-guess the doctor. Tomorrow you'll have trouble even hobbling around. Incidentally, if you aren't in bed by the time I'm back with the water, I'll put you there." His last statement was made just as dispassionately as the rest, but a flicker of a smile played over his face before he disappeared into the bathroom.

For a second, Krista smiled unwillingly in response. It would be fun to put his words to the test, she decided, toying with the belt of her robe. She could sit defiantly on the edge of the bed and dare him to carry through with his threat when he came back into the room; tell him that she didn't intend to be sent to bed like a child, and sit back to see what happened.

Then, as she heard the clink of glass on the tile counter in the bath, her spirit of defiance died. She hurriedly peeled off her robe and stepped out of her satin scuffs as she wondered what in the world was the matter with her. Theirs wasn't an ordinary honeymoon in which such byplay was common.

She had just sighed and pulled the sheet up to her chin as Ryan reentered the bedroom, carrying the glass of water.

Evidently he overheard her. He smiled sympathetically. "What's the matter, honey? Aches and pains catching up with you?"

Krista had watched him adopt that kindly impersonal manner with little old lady visitors to the zoo, and it triggered a violent reaction. "I wish you wouldn't use that tone of voice," she complained, snatching the glass from him so carelessly that she succeeded in spilling some water onto the sheet. "Oh, damn! Now see what I've done!"

"Take it easy," Ryan soothed, sitting down on the edge of the mattress beside her. "Want to move to the other bed?"

Krista wriggled into a more upright position and eyed him strangely. "Because of the water, you mean?"

"Of course. What do you think I meant?" He sounded as if he were holding onto his patience with great difficulty.

That gave Krista a perverse feeling of satisfaction. "The dampness won't bother me. It's sort of refreshing." She shook the sheet carelessly. "Is the air-conditioning working?"

Ryan frowned as he nodded. "It's on full force. Look, Krista . . . be reasonable. You probably have a low temperature, so you can't get chilled." He stood up and turned down the other bed. "Move over here."

"But what will you do?" Krista asked, thoroughly enjoying the situation.

"By the time I'm ready to go to bed . . . that sheet will be dry, so it doesn't matter in the least." He bent over the foot of the bed and transferred her robe, then swept the sheet back and pulled her upright. "Come on, woman—move."

As she stood up, Krista became aware of the transparency of her nightgown, and it was only by exercising great self-control that she managed to make the transfer gracefully instead of following her instincts and leaping into the other bed.

She waited until she was finally settled under the covers and had swallowed her pills before she gathered enough confidence to meet Ryan's gaze again.

His kindly avuncular manner, she noted with surprise, had disappeared somewhere during the transfer. Now, he was standing well away from her—looking as if he'd just discovered a lioness in his pygmy goat enclosure.

Slowly Krista put the glass on the table and leaned gracefully back against her pillows. "You can't imagine how good this bed feels," she said. Ryan's eyes narrowed as he stared down at her and she let her own eyelids flutter down. "You don't have to turn off the lights now," she told him. "They won't keep me from going to sleep if you want to stay in the room."

Ryan took a deep breath; it appeared to be an effort. "Never mind. I think I'll go down and take a walk. I need some exercise." He approached the bed light with as much care as if it had been shooting out sparks. After he'd turned it off, he stood by the side of the bed uncertainly. "You'll be all right here by yourself?" That time he didn't add any casual endearment, Krista noted.

She thought a moment before answering. Then she smiled in the darkness and said softly, "I'll be fine. You go enjoy your walk." She heard his footsteps move slowly out to the hallway before she spoke again. "Ryan?"

He came back quickly. "What is it, Kris?" His voice sounded vibrant and eager.

"I hope I don't disturb you tonight. With my aches and pains, I mean."

There was a moment of silence before he said irritably, "I don't expect your aches and pains to bother me one damned bit." Then the door slammed behind him.

As she turned over and burrowed her head into the pillow, Krista's smile widened. It was, she thought, an entirely satisfactory answer.

Chapter *FIVE*

She awoke the next morning to find Ryan bending over the edge of the bed and shaking her shoulder.

"Rise and shine, Kris . . . time to wake up and see how you feel. The waiter will be bringing your breakfast in a few minutes."

Krista groaned as she pushed her hair from her eyes and tried to focus on the leather travel alarm by the head of the bed. "What time is it, for heaven's sake? It feels like dawn." Then, as she opened her eyes wider and saw his brown slacks and sport shirt, she added confusedly, "Didn't you go to bed at all?"

"I certainly did. The evidence is right there." He nodded toward the rumpled bed behind him. "You were sleeping so soundly that you didn't even hear the alarm when I shut it off at eight."

She frowned at that . . . not sure that she approved of the picture he was painting of her recumbent form.

Evidently he was reading her mind again. "You looked like an exhausted infant," he said, grinning, "with a far sweeter disposition than I've noticed during your waking hours. C'mon, try getting vertical." He tossed her robe to her from the foot of the bed and tactfully went over to draw the curtain covering the balcony door while she got out of bed and put it on. He only turned around when he heard her indrawn gasp as she started to walk toward the bath. "Can you navigate by yourself?" he asked with concern as he noted her painful hobbling.

"As soon as I move around a little, I'll be OK," she assured him. "Is there time for a hot shower before breakfast?"

"If there isn't, we'll just send down for more coffee. Take your time." He slid the glass door aside. "How about eating on the balcony? We might as well absorb some of the local color."

"It sounds good. I'll hurry getting dressed." She wondered why he had decided to abandon the dining room this morning. Probably he felt he should watch over his invalid wife.

"You can dress after breakfast. We might as well enjoy a *few* of the benefits of the married state, and that robe of yours is very fetching." He came back into the room. "I've discovered I like pale blue satin lapels."

She flushed but still looked doubtful. "*You're* dressed."

"Well, I didn't think you'd find an unshaven husband very exciting across the breakfast table." He grinned. "Besides, I can't claim an invalid state. Now get your shower over or I'll drink all the coffee while I'm waiting."

After that threat, Krista stayed under the hot water just long enough to ease her aching muscles before toweling herself briskly. Fortunately, her long robe covered the bruises which had appeared overnight. She was a symphony in blue, green, and yellow, she decided whimsically. Then she took especial care with her hair and her lipstick, deciding that Ryan might as well discover a few more benefits of the married state. She didn't bother to rationalize why she went to all the trouble—she merely added a spray of 4711 cologne as a final fragrant touch and strolled out trying to look as if breakfast with an attractive man on a sunny balcony happened *all* the time.

Ryan's lifted eyebrows testified to the success of her appearance, although he didn't say anything. He did, however, settle her into the wrought iron balcony chair as if she were visiting royalty.

"You look as if you feel much better." His comment came after he was settled in his chair again and was pouring her coffee.

"Never underestimate the effects of a little hot water," she said lightly, sipping her iced orange juice. "Mmmm . . . this tastes wonderful."

"Morocco oranges are a premium crop . . . much sweeter than the European varieties, they claim." He put her coffee cup within reach and then topped his. "The croissants look better this morning, too. One of the French cooks must have stayed in Marrakesh. Only tremendous willpower kept me from finishing the lot before you arrived." He passed the plate to her and then helped himself. "I hope you appreciate it."

"Oh, I do." Her eyes sparkled with enjoyment as she looked down on the patio in front of them. "Isn't this the most gorgeous place? With that row of palm trees and those red and white flower beds surrounding that elegant swimming pool."

"It's plush, all right," he admitted. "Like most of Africa, life here is a study in contrasts. But it's too pretty a day for sober subjects . . . let's just enjoy it as it comes." The laughter wrinkles at the corners of his eyes deepened. "Anybody who couldn't enjoy this place should have his head examined. I'd like to stay a month. It's the last word in twentieth-century luxury."

She nodded as she pushed her empty juice glass away and watched a white-robed gardener clear insects from the pool with a long-handled dip net. From the languor of his movements, he was evidently enjoying the sunny morning calm as well. Krista sighed softly and pulled her robe around her. "Even the prospect of visiting a zoo doesn't sound as tempting as usual. If that sounds like heresy, I'm sorry. . . ."

"Don't worry . . . the news will never get back to your crusty employer."

"I've never accused you of being crusty. . . ."

He grinned without repentance. "Your memory's slipping. What about the time I objected to your having fourteen fawns in the nursery at once?"

"I called you stubborn maybe. But not crusty."

"I'll let you win—this time." He finished the last bite of his croissant and leaned back in his chair. "Anyhow—I've been thinking that there's no reason for us to go to the zoo this morning—we can do that in the late part of the afternoon. How about taking in the big central souk now before it gets too hot?"

Krista's eyes widened. "You mean—change the tour schedule? What will Hamid say?"

Ryan's face wore an amused expression. "Why does that matter? After all, Kris, he's just our guide—not our mentor."

"But what about the others? Eve . . . and the Westons?"

"What about them?" he asked calmly. "We have different schedules, so I can't see why we have to be herded through the souk together as if we were a bunch of schoolchildren."

Krista was so delighted at this casual dismissal of Eve from their plans that she almost choked on her coffee. "It sounds fine," she managed finally. "I'd love to wander through the market on our own. There's supposed to be a fabulous storyteller in the big square. . . ."

"You'll just have to enjoy his gestures if we're alone." He looked thoughtful. "Maybe we could use Hamid as a translator, after all."

"Oh, no. We don't need anyone." Her denial spilled out. "If I want to learn about Arabic folklore, I can ask Hamid when he translates the proverbs for me."

Ryan's forehead creased in a frown. "Which proverbs are you talking about?"

She gestured with her free hand. "It's nothing important. Hamid gave me a little volume of sayings as sort of a 'Welcome to Morocco' present. He promised to tell me what they meant later on."

"That was nice of him. Actually he seems extremely conscientious for a tour guide."

"I know . . . but that's one reason why it will be nice to be on our own this morning. I'm getting stuffed with vital statistics that every tourist should know."

"And today you'd just like to spend money."

Her lips curved in response to his taunt. "That sounds like a very husbandly remark, Dr. Talbot. I didn't plan on being extravagant. Or not terribly extravagant," she amended.

His chuckle surfaced to laughter. "You don't have to explain. The only rule I'm making is that any big purchases have to be mailed. Otherwise, at this rate, we'll have to buy a donkey to carry the loot. That basket of yours looks pregnant already. And don't tell me that I'm the one who bought the whisk broom," he added severely. "I'm well aware of the lapse. Of course, we could drop it in a wastebasket and solve the problem. . . ."

"You wouldn't," she said, scandalized.

"OK, I wouldn't. We'll keep it for a fond memento . . . but no more lapses. Now"—he glanced at his watch—"you'd better get dressed. I'd just as soon miss the rest of the bunch when we go through the lobby and avoid explanations. OK?"

"Very much so." She got up feeling like a new woman. Even her sore muscles didn't protest too vigorously. "Would you like to see that book of proverbs while you're waiting?"

"I'll look at it later," he said, following her back to the bedroom. "Right now, I'll call the Tourism Office and try to reach Hamid, so he won't be searching for us."

"Then I'll dress in the bathroom," Krista said casually as she rummaged in her suitcase for a blouse to go with her flared turquoise skirt.

"OK." Ryan sat down on the edge of his bed and reached for the telephone. "Sing out if you need help."

"Thanks, I will." Krista was still smiling when she disappeared into the bath. From the casualness of his tone, Ryan might have been an old married man. She thought about it carefully as she dressed, and it was a very pensive young woman who rejoined him later on.

The large square which was the entrance to Marrakesh's famed souk, or marketplace, was jammed with people when they arrived.

"We should have come by camel instead of a taxi," Krista told Ryan as he finished paying the driver of the mini-cab and they crossed a crowded sidewalk.

"Camels, donkeys, horse carts, taxicabs . . ." he

said, looking around and then taking her elbow to dodge away from a loaded burro. "Apparently anything goes. The only thing that's missing in this jam is a Rolls Royce."

"That and a couple of Fire Department Aid cars. ... I'd need some help if I wore those getups." She was staring wide-eyed at the attire of the people around her. Despite the broiling sunshine, each man and woman was muffled from head to toe in a heavy cloth djellabah. In addition, most of the women wore yashmaks, a veiling which left only their eyes uncovered. Krista shook her head wonderingly. She was bare-legged, wearing a thin blouse over a cotton skirt plus the absolute minimum in nylon underthings, but she could feel the heat as if a broiler oven were just below the concrete. "Look at that man," she marveled, nodding to an old gentleman sitting cross-legged by a display of brass belts. "He even has a wool sweater on under his djellabah. I don't see how he can stand it."

Ryan nodded and reached for his handkerchief to mop his forehead. "I know what you mean. Let's get across the square and into the souk, where there's some shade."

They threaded their way around the circle of tourists who were photographing five water-sellers in their bright red costumes with brass cups jangling from their shirtfronts and waistlines.

Krista looked around, puzzled. "There isn't any water to go with the cups, why do they bother?"

"It's strictly a show for the tourists these days since the people can get their own water at the fountain in the souk." Ryan was looking regretfully over his shoulder at the colorful group. "Damn! I wish I'd brought my camera. Oh, well, it's nice not to have to carry it."

"Look! That must be the storyteller." Krista pulled him to a stop at the edge of a wide circle of Arabs who were avidly listening to a turbaned man in a djellabah. He shouted hoarsely at the crowd as he waved his arms and then suddenly he sprawled at full-length on the concrete, obviously dramatizing the climax of his story. Both Krista and Ryan stared as he rolled in pseudo-agony on the dusty pavement and then leaped to his feet again and stretched his hands over his head.

"My God—in this heat, too," Ryan murmured. "It makes me tired to even watch him." He glanced down at Krista. "Had enough?"

She nodded and let herself be led along. "Television was never like this. Hey! There's a snake charmer over there. . . ."

"I think we can skip that," Ryan said firmly. "It's strictly a gimmick. . . ."

Her lips twitched. "So are belly dancers, but Hamid apparently thinks we shouldn't miss them."

"He claims it's a vital part of the native culture. . . ."

"And of course, cobras aren't native to Morocco; they're Indian. That makes the difference."

"Exactly." His grin broadened. "If you're so keen on reptiles, you can spend your time studying the snakes at the zoo this afternoon."

"While you'll do your part and study the belly dancers at the casino tonight." She kept a straight face with difficulty. "I think it's only fair to warn you that you'll be chaperoned every inch of the way. I'm feeling much better suddenly. . . ."

Ryan heaved a mock sigh. "There's an old Arab proverb about wives . . . they say 'the bird is small but the beak is sharp.' "

"Well, you can always try to shove me into the lion's cage this afternoon."

He pretended to consider it. "I don't think they feed Christians to the lions these days—even in a Moslem country. Nope—I'll have to think of something else."

Two hours later as they left the final reed-covered alleyway of the souk and made their way back to the street, Krista took off her wide-brimmed straw hat and fanned herself with it. "You won't have to do anything drastic to get rid of me—a few more minutes in this sun and I'll just melt away. Do you suppose we can ever find a cab to get back to the hotel?"

"If we can't—we'll buy a camel." Ryan was trying to shove the leather belt he'd purchased into his back pants pocket, but had to give up.

"Here . . . I'll put it in my purse. There should be room if you'll take your sunglasses," she said, fishing them out and handing them to him.

"Er . . . thanks." He looked slightly embarrassed. "I didn't mean to load you down, but they don't make enough pockets in men's clothes these days."

"One of the unpublicized virtues of matrimony," she said, enjoying his discomfort. "Now I know why husbands buy their wives big purses."

His eyes gleamed with laughter before he shoved his sunglasses on. "Or baskets in Tangier."

"I was too polite to mention it."

"How about something cold to drink as a partial payment," he suggested and then reneged as he saw the sun beating down on the soft-drink vendor's umbrella. "On second thought, let's wait until we get back to the hotel. OK?"

She nodded and followed behind him across the

sidewalk toward a taxi stand on a crowded side
street where a single cab was discharging a fare.
She watched the veiled woman passenger accept
her change and then gather her plastic shopping
bag in one hand and grasp a toddler with the
other before making her way through the crowds.
Nearby, a seller of goat's milk crouched on his
haunches, serving his customers in the shade of a
mud wall.

Ryan followed her glance. "If you want bread
and milk, he even furnishes that," he said softly.
"See the woman crouching beside him behind that
piece of canvas? She has a stack of bread to keep
him supplied."

Krista watched the milk seller cut a circle of
flat bread in half, hollow the center of it with his
fingers, and then apply a kind of butter with
those same fingers before handing it to the
waiting customer. Wordlessly, she looked back to
Ryan.

"At least it cuts down on the dish washing."
He bundled her toward the idling cab. "And
they'd probably flinch at some of our hamburger
drive-ins." He helped her in and gave the driver
the name of the hotel. Then, seeing Krista still
stare through the back window as they drove off,
he added, "That eating place isn't as bad as one I
saw in Macao. They were drying sharks' fins on
the curb with a solid layer of flies on top." He
shook his head reminiscently. "Haven't eaten
shark's fin soup since."

Krista said faintly, "Now I know why everybody
says, 'Don't eat it if it can't be peeled, uncorked,
or cooked.' "

"Forget it. They looked healthier than we do."
Ryan gestured toward an open lot where four
camels and two donkeys were tethered. "Sure you

don't want a ride? You're missing a good bet there."

Krista grinned at him, her good humor restored. "If I got on top of one of those, I'd have more bruises still. Besides, I've already tried the houdah on the elephant at home. I'll be glad to wait while you go 'round the block, though."

"No, thanks ... not in this sun." As the driver turned right down the boulevard under a magnificent canopy of jacaranda trees in bloom, he went on, "Do you feel like visiting the zoo this afternoon? There's no reason you can't rest at the hotel."

"And gather my strength for the casino tonight?" Her eyes glinted with mischief. "I'd hate to miss either appointment. If Hamid's going to drive us to the zoo, there shouldn't be any transportation delays."

"I guess you're right. He insisted on going when I told him about our change in plans this morning." Ryan stroked his jaw thoughtfully. "S'funny that Hamid's so keen on zoos." He let his glance rest on her profile. "Or maybe he's keen on your company."

"Me?" Her voice was an astonished squeak. "You're crazy."

"Well, he was certainly curious as to whether you were going along. Once he heard you were— then he volunteered to drive us. I think you've collected an admirer."

Krista refused to take him seriously. "You'll probably discover that he's a frustrated animal lover ... like our volunteers at Woodsea who want to work in the nursery."

"I don't blame them; sometimes animals are easier to handle than people and a darned sight more predictable."

Krista started to giggle.

"Now what?" Ryan asked.

"I was just thinking how predictable the polar bears were this spring"—she chuckled—"when they insisted on doing their courting out by the moat in front of everybody."

"You wouldn't be laughing," he said darkly, "if you'd had to write all the letters of apology to teachers of visiting school groups. Remind me to change their tour route next spring."

"I'll do that."

"Of course, there is another possibility. . . ."

"What's that?"

"I could always buy a leather screen. Very versatile things—screens."

Krista darted a startled look at him before noting with relief that they were driving into the entrance of the hotel.

"Saved again," Ryan muttered in her ear as he leaned forward to open the door when the taxi drew to a stop.

Krista hopped out and paused just long enough to say, "I'll see you up in the room. Frankly, I can't wait to change and get into the swimming pool," before leaving him in financial negotiations with the driver.

Evidently he found something else to occupy him besides paying their taxi fare, because he still hadn't appeared by the time she had changed into her swimsuit.

Krista frowned slightly at his absence and then went over to the mirror to check her appearance; the orange-flowered swimsuit wasn't precisely a bikini but it clung tightly enough in all the accepted places to be a distant cousin. It was definitely whistle bait ... even with a scraped knee and some bruises in evidence.

She picked up her petal bathing cap, pushed her sunglasses on her nose, and folded a towel over her arm before going out into the hallway. After hesitating for a minute, she pulled the door tightly closed behind her—hoping as she walked down the pool stairs that Ryan would appear with a key before she went back in.

He arrived at the pool a half hour later just in time to watch her dive from the middle board—with more enthusiasm than athletic grace.

As she surfaced, he was treading water calmly beside her. He didn't say anything when she shook the water from her face. Indeed it was his pointed lack of comment that made her flare.

"It wasn't *that* bad, was it?"

"Of course not. Besides, every swimmer belly flops now and then," he said reasonably.

"Thanks very much." She glared at him and stroked her way to the side of the pool. "You don't have to be so graphic."

"And you shouldn't be so sensitive." He moved easily through the water beside her. "What are you getting out for?"

"Because I'm tired . . . and because you've made me feel like Clorinda in her pool," she said, referring to the fattest occupant of Woodsea's hippo colony.

Ryan laughed as he watched her climb up out of the pool and reach for her towel. "Clorinda couldn't compete with your measurements if she went on a crash diet for years," he assured her. "You should sit on the edge of a swimming pool more often."

"Exactly what I say," Jeff replied, coming around the deep end and surveying her admiringly. "The Arabs might like their females on the hefty side but your wife could change their minds."

"Sorry. That's one cultural exchange I'm not allowing," Ryan said firmly.

Jeff grinned. "I thought you'd feel that way. Don't worry, it wasn't an official suggestion." He dropped his towel on a nearby lounge, yanked up his dark blue swim trunks, and put a cautious foot in the water. They saw a beatific expression spread over his face. "Ah ... perfect. This is the life." Then, holding his nose, he calmly stepped off the side of the pool. He came up sputtering seconds later and turned on his back. "I meant to ask where you'd disappeared this morning," he continued as if there'd been no interruption. "Eve was beating the bushes all around the hotel."

"Can't imagine why." Ryan hoisted himself onto the side of the pool near the lounge where Krista was drying her hair. "Toss me my towel, will you? Thanks." He wiped his face before turning back to Jeff. "Actually we just reversed our schedule. It makes more sense to go to the zoo this afternoon rather than struggle through that crowd in the souks."

"Well, I hope you don't mind company on your trip," Jeff said. "Hamid told the rest of the bunch; they decided to cut their shopping short after lunch and take in the zoo, as well."

Ryan merely raised his eyebrows. "They're apt to be disappointed—this is a very small private zoo. Naturally it can't compete with the more lavish metropolitan outlays."

Krista sat still but her thoughts were racing furiously. If Ryan were disappointed, he was hiding it admirably. Perhaps, she thought disconsolately, he was even welcoming the thought of Eve's company after sparring with her all morning.

The entire patio suddenly lost its glamour,

despite its picture postcard appearance with brightly colored lounges and umbrella tables dotting the tiled apron of the huge pool. Even the towering palms with their wide girdles of purple bougainvillea on the trunks lost their flamboyant charm, and the fragrant breeze from the glossy lemon trees screening the tennis courts went unnoticed.

Krista's lips drooped and she got up quietly.

"Where are you going?" Ryan wanted to know.

"Back to the room. After all my exercise this morning, a little peace and quiet sounds inviting," she lied with a bright smile.

His glance changed to one of concern. Poor Ryan, she thought suddenly. Saddled with a flighty wife when he'd obviously prefer being on his own.

"You'll be down for lunch, won't you?" he was asking.

"Heavens, yes ... I'll probably be first in line. Even though the Moroccans don't follow the Spanish timetable for food, it seems hours since breakfast."

Jeff heaved his bulk over to the edge of the pool and nodded. "You don't have to tell me! If coffee and rolls are barely enough for a sylph like you—imagine how I feel." He looked comically down to his thick waistline.

Ryan smiled absently and turned back to Krista. "After your rest—put on something cool for lunch. We'll take off for the zoo from there. And don't forget your hat," he added peremptorily when she moved away. "There'll still be plenty of afternoon sun."

"All right." She continued walking.

"Wait a second." He caught up with her and

fished their room key from the pocket of his trunks. "You'll need this."

"Thanks. I must have been thinking of something else."

Ryan noticed that her smile didn't reach her eyes. "Or someone," he said softly. "Do me a favor, Kris—and stop thinking. You're coming up with all the wrong answers."

Her puzzled glance followed him all the way back to the pool before she turned and trudged toward the room.

For a zoologist, he was becoming terribly cryptic all of a sudden. Probably that was why Eve understood him so well—psychologists were supposed to be experts in human behavior.

Krista thrust the key into the lock on their door with an irritated jab. What a pity she'd only specialized in animals ... that was why she understood Eve's behavior so well. The woman was just like a feline who played and performed for her audience, batting at her handler with unsheathed claws—only to yawn and pad away after she'd drawn blood.

Chapter SIX

The Toubkal Zoo and Botanical Garden was a twenty-minute ride south of Marrakesh over a dusty gravel road. When Hamid finally drew up before the entrance, he shut off the ignition on the van and turned to Ryan and Krista apologetically. "I'm sorry—it isn't much." He waved an expressive hand at the main gate.

They stared past it to the short fence of prickly pear cactus where a sign giving the admittance fees hung crookedly. Still farther beyond, two blind men sat on their haunches in the shade of the eucalyptus windbreak. A few coins in the dust in front of them gave mute appeal to the visitors passing by. On the other side of the path, a vendor selling nuts in twists of newspaper doubled as a ticket seller as well.

"It is expensive to maintain a zoo," Hamid started to explain, "and the families in charge of this one would like to sell their interests. Their father, who started it many years ago, died just recently."

"You don't have to apologize," Ryan said. "There's never enough money in the budget for any zoo . . . even when it's a city's responsibility. As for a private one . . ." He shook his head.

Hamid looked relieved. "I knew you'd understand. Unfortunately, the rest of your group will be disappointed. That's why I tried to discourage their coming. But no—nothing would do but they must join us here when they finish touring the market square. I can't think why."

I can, Krista thought to herself, remembering Eve's vivacity at lunch when she was quizzing Ryan about his job.

"Well, they won't have long." Ryan glanced at his watch and then opened the van door. "This place will be closing shortly after they arrive." He helped Krista out and reached back on the seat for his camera.

"You go ahead," Hamid told them. "I'll take care of the admission fees. Would you like to meet the director right away?"

"I'd rather wait until we've looked around," Ryan said. "Probably he only speaks Arabic or French, so any conversation will be difficult . . . at least as far as I'm concerned." He was unzipping his camera case and putting the strap around his neck.

"I can take notes for you," Krista offered.

"Fine." He was squinting thoughtfully down the main entrance path where a few children were hanging over waist-high fences to peer at two waterfowl enclosures. "Actually—there's not much for us to do here. Some of those gardens are nice." He indicated a grove of palms to their left. "And it wouldn't hurt to have a record of their planting."

"If you don't need me right now, I'll rejoin you in about a half hour," Hamid said, as he returned and handed Ryan their ticket stubs. "I have some business I should attend to."

"Of course. Where do you want to meet?"

"There is a refreshment stand outside the zoo office. . . ."

"Sounds good," Ryan said briskly. "We'll be there."

"A half hour should be plenty here," Krista said as the two of them were walking up the main path to the exhibits. "I think this whole place couldn't cover more than two acres. Golly ... it really needs some maintenance." She wrinkled her nose as they caught the fragrance of a duck pond next to the path.

"The small fry don't mind a few minor inconveniences," Ryan said with a grin. He indicated three barefooted youngsters in shorts and T-shirts who had their noses up against the wire fence. The veiled woman wearing a heavy gray cotton djellabah who was walking with them was obviously enjoying the exhibit as well.

"Let's move on ... or at least get away from the windward side," Krista suggested. "Besides, I think I see their feline cages up that path to the left." She pulled him along past a young courting couple who appeared far more interested in each other than the camel enclosure which was next to the duck pond.

Ryan hung back to glance at them and then he shook his head, chuckling.

"Now what?" Krista wanted to know.

"I was just thinking that the young bloods in this country need a lot of luck. That djellabah covers her like a small tent and her veil muffles most everything from the neck up. With that kind of camouflage, what chance does a man have?"

"I'll bet they manage somehow," Krista's tone was tart.

Ryan strolled on. "Well, if they don't—there's always the yearly trade-in at Imichil."

Krista searched for a scathing reply and then

caught sight of his grin. "I should have known you wouldn't forget that," she said. "Why the sudden interest in people? You've always concentrated on animals before."

"All part of the vital statistics. A man has to keep an open mind," he drawled. A minute later he had stopped to survey three dromedaries who were standing in the middle of a dusty pen looking profoundly bored. "Camels in a Morocco zoo," he mused. "They must have a surplus of these fellows."

Krista's attention was caught by a French-lettered placard nailed on a pillar nearby. "I don't think so. Look—that sign tells what surplus animals they have for sale."

"I'll be damned. Belgian hares, white pigeons, peahens, and hamsters. I've never seen that before."

"Can you imagine what would happen at home if we started listing our spare raccoons and badgers?" Krista giggled. "The city fathers and ecologists would be on our necks in a minute."

They wandered on past a stand of bamboo which separated the feline cages from the rest of the enclosures.

"Oh dear," Krista said as they investigated some small barred cages containing their lions and leopards. "The poor things don't have any place for exercise at all."

"Well, it hasn't affected their appetite," Ryan said.

Two lions were intently watching the keeper select haunches of raw meat from a nearby wheelbarrow. The man pushed the meat through the bars, keeping a sharp lookout for the cage's occupants as he did. There was a brief skirmish while the two cats settled who was to have first choice, and then they fell on the meat hungrily.

Krista sighed and turned away.

"Cheer up," Ryan said as they walked on, "at least those cats know where their next meal is coming from."

"And the cage *was* clean," she agreed, looking a little brighter. "All right—I'll be thankful for all blessings. Do we have time to go down this other path?"

Ryan nodded as she hesitated by a narrow trail winding through a grove of eucalyptus trees. "I wonder what they have down there. Too bad we can't read the signs."

Krista smiled at the Arabic placard tacked on a tree trunk. "Maybe it's advertising the latest cure for sinus trouble."

"More likely one for sunstroke," Ryan said, mopping his forehead with a handkerchief. "God, it's hot." He pulled her to a stop. "Do you hear what I hear?"

"Sounds like a pack of hounds. It can't be anything very big—there's just a row of tiny cages with runs attached." She hurried to catch up with Ryan. "Oh, for heaven's sake. . . ." She stopped short as she identified the occupants of the first cage.

"Cocker spaniels," Ryan said dazedly. "And the next cage has two boxers. . . ."

"Followed by a pair of German shepherds and two collies." Krista didn't know whether to laugh or cry. "It's an exhibit of purebred domestic dogs." She knelt down by the wire enclosure and reached through to pet the muzzle of a friendly little honey-colored cocker.

"Well, it makes sense." Ryan was rubbing the back of his neck as he stared around him. "Dogs of this type are a novelty here. It's an inexpensive exhibit and Moroccan youngsters must enjoy it. . . ."

"I know, and I'm used to seeing dingoes and wild dogs in cages, but cockers and collies ..." Krista shook her head, gave the dog a final pat, and stood up. "I'd like to open all the gates."

Ryan nodded with sympathy. "At least the runs are adequate and probably they're as spoiled as most of our pets." As Krista continued to look unconvinced, he took her elbow and steered her back up the path. "C'mon. It's time we were meeting Hamid. Then we'd better find the zoo director and exchange amenities."

Krista hung back as they approached the office quarters. She could see Hamid already in a discussion with a heavy-set man who had made a token gesture toward formality by donning a mismatched suit coat over an open-throated shirt. He was waving his hands as he carried on in a rapid spate of French.

"Ryan—you go ahead," she said. "My French is miserable and, honestly, I'd rather go wait in the shade by the van. He'll probably want to show you some more exhibits and, frankly, I'm whacked."

"Are you sure?" Ryan asked, concerned.

"Positive."

"Well ..." He hesitated and then his frown smoothed out. "You won't be on your own. It looks as if the rest of the bunch are coming through the main gate now."

Krista took a tighter grip on her purse and stifled a sigh. There was no point in telling him that she'd much rather be alone than have to make conversation with the Westons, Herb, and Eve. "I'll probably catch up with them a little later," she told him hurriedly. "Right now, I'll wander down this side path. There must be some trumpeter swans by the sound of things." She smiled and gave him a casual wave. "See you back at the bus."

Ryan frowned again as he stared after her trim figure. Now why had she beat such a hasty retreat? Even if she hadn't wanted to meet the zoo director, he could have installed her at one of the metal tables next to the refreshment bar with a cold drink. He took another look at the tables with the accumulation of sandy grit on top of them and grimaced. Maybe Krista was right.

"Dr. Talbot, this way, please." Hamid was beckoning imperiously, and Ryan sighed again before walking over to the two men.

Hamid performed the introductions, and then as the rest of the group approached, he went through the necessary formalities again. As soon as he saw that most of them were sufficiently conversant in French to get by, he drew back and unobtrusively strolled up the narrow path that Krista had taken.

He found her in a shady patch near the entrance leaning against the trunk of a eucalyptus tree and staring absently at a pair of peacocks preening themselves.

She gave an audible start as his presence finally penetrated, and she swung around. "Hamid! You startled me!" Her hand fluttered up to her throat. "I didn't expect anyone along here."

"Your husband and the others were doing very well with the director, so I thought I'd find some peace and quiet as well." His smile was a flash of white against his tanned skin. "It's very pleasant here—you've chosen the best part of the grounds."

Krista looked around as if seeing it for the first time. "I suppose you're right." Obviously her thoughts had wandered far from the scenery.

Hamid decided to skip further diplomatic skirmishing. "Mrs. Talbot—I have a favor to beg of you. It's nothing difficult," he said in a reassuring tone. "I just wanted to ask you to look up a friend of mine when you go to Switzerland. You *are* going to Switzerland next, aren't you?"

"Why, yes." Krista made an effort to pull her thoughts into line. "There's a seminar at the zoo in Basel next week. Dr. Talbot ..." She remembered suddenly that wives hadn't referred to their spouses in the third person since Victorian times. "I mean ... my husband is one of the speakers," she managed finally.

"I thought so. Isn't that quite an honor for such a young man?"

"Oh, yes! Ryan's achieved wonderful results on some endangered species, and our primate section is ..." She broke off, puzzled. "I didn't know *you* were interested in that kind of thing."

"To be truthful, my friend is particularly fond of zoological parks. He's studying for a degree in biology at the University in Heidelberg, but at the moment he's on a holiday in Switzerland." Hamid paused and went on. "Actually, he is a fine Arabic scholar as well, and if you liked, he could translate that booklet I gave you. Most of us enjoy showing off our meager talents."

"Of course, we'd be pleased to meet him. We'll have to set an exact time and place later on." She pulled her hat brim lower as she glanced at him against the sun. "I thought *you* were going to translate that book for me."

Hamid looked nervously around their deserted clearing. "My schedule has been changed, Mrs. Talbot. The way things are, I can't plan ahead."

"Of course, I understand." Krista wondered

why he was choosing to be so obscure. If he didn't want to bother with the translation, he could have found a simpler excuse.

He was shaking his head. "Dear lady—you have no conception of our problems. No foreigner could have. I don't mean to be rude," he added hastily. "Both you and your husband have shown me great courtesy. That's why I'm warning you now. . . ."

Her head came up. "Warning me!"

"That's right." He glanced over his shoulder again. "You and Dr. Talbot would do well to leave this country as quickly as possible."

"But the tour isn't over for two more days. . . ."

"That's of no importance. I suggest you cut your visit short. Later, you can return. . . ."

Krista was amused at his casual proposals. "Good heavens, Hamid. We can't afford to commute from Europe to North Africa. That doesn't make sense at all."

"It makes sense to leave a place if you're in physical danger," he told her. "What good is all your knowledge if you don't live to use it?"

Her eyes widened at the thinly veiled threat. "I don't understand you. What danger? When we've been stopped at the roadblocks, the soldiers haven't even bothered to search us. They couldn't have been more polite. I don't think they've anything against foreigners."

"I'm not talking about all foreigners, Mrs. Talbot. I'm talking about you. . . ."

"Well, if you're trying to frighten me, you're going about it the wrong way. I'm not impressed," Krista said, wishing she'd stayed with the others in the group. Right then she would have welcomed the sight of the Westons or even Eve coming toward her. "You'll have to speak to my husband about things like this. Not that he'll pay any attention. After all, we haven't suffered so far. . . ." Her words broke off at the memory of her plunge down the dark stairway in Fez. If that had been a deliberate attempt to injure her rather than an accidental encounter . . . She drew in her breath sharply and stared again at Hamid. "You're talking about Fez, aren't you? You told a different story at the time."

He shrugged. "What could I say to the others? And how could we prove anything? You were another careless foreigner in high-heeled shoes. A pretty blonde stranger who should be grateful that she merely hurt her knee and didn't damage her neck. *Inn Sha Allah*—my people would say."

"Well, I'll tell my husband," Krista said, clinging to the thought of Ryan like a stout timber in a storm. "But he's going to think I've been out in the sun too long. Wanting to cut our visit short because of a fall down the stairs." She turned to Hamid abruptly. "If *you* could tell him that there's going to be trouble . . ."

"Oh, no!" Hamid pulled back as if the bluebottle fly buzzing between them had suddenly changed into a wasp. "That's impossible, Mrs. Talbot. I would lose my job immediately if my superiors heard of such a rumor. Any persuasion has to come from you. And as for facts"—his voice was scornful—"what beautiful woman needs them? It's obvious that your husband will do whatever you ask—I've seen the way he looks at you."

After such a comment, Krista was sure that the guide's imagination had got the better of him. Ryan's most intimate looks were hardly the kind to move mountains—let alone cut tours short. "I'll remember what you've said," she told him noncommittally, "but I can't promise anything."

"Any precautions will be wise," he said, falling into step beside her as she walked back toward the main path. "I sincerely hope there won't be any trouble, but sometimes innocent people get hurt in our political maneuverings. . . ."

"Well, at least I can promise that we'll meet your friend in Switzerland," she said, while wondering what he meant. "Do you have an address or telephone number?"

"Neither will be necessary. He spends all his spare time at the zoo these days and he'll get in touch with you when you visit there. You'll be with Dr. Talbot when he speaks at the seminar, won't you?"

"Of course. Does your friend have a name?"

He smiled then. "I thought I had mentioned it. Actually it's a very long one . . . Abdellatif Amid Khaoulan. Too much for you to remember. Just call him Abdell."

Krista nodded and pulled up as they rejoined the main path of the zoo near the entrance. She watched a young Arab girl hurry past to greet two older women, kissing their hands with charming affection and receiving loving smiles in return. It was a pity, she thought, that some Moroccan customs couldn't be adopted by their politicians.

"Do you want to wait in the bus or would you rather rejoin your husband?" Hamid was asking.

"I'm not sure. . . ." Just then she looked up the path the other way and saw Jeff and Ryan coming toward them with Eve cozily sandwiched in between. While she watched, Eve laughed at one of Ryan's remarks and went up on her tiptoes to plant a kiss on his cheek.

Krista abruptly turned toward the bus with

Hamid hurrying along beside her, his silence testifying to the effectiveness of Eve's gesture. As he unlocked the van door, Krista noted with bitter amusement that no further references were made to Dr. Talbot's affection for his wife.

For the main part, the ride back to Marrakesh was made in preoccupied silence. The Westons were apparently exhausted by the afternoon heat, and Herb Freeman was content to sit beside Hamid, fanning himself with his visored cap. Eve stared dreamily out the window, and Jeff, after attempting to start a conversation with Krista and receiving only monosyllabic replies, sat with his eyes closed. Ryan's face still wore a puzzled frown after Krista's cool greeting, but he chose not to pursue her reasons just then. Instead, he occupied himself by winding off the finished film in his camera and making notes on an old envelope. Krista glanced at him from under half-closed lids and wondered how he could look so innocent.

Then she deliberately turned and concentrated on the back of Hamid's sleek head. For the first time since Eve's gesture, she recalled the guide's warning and felt like laughing aloud at his urgings. It would have been difficult to tell Ryan of her suspicions at any time without feeling an utter fool. Now, he'd regard her suggestion to shorten their trip as merely a flare-up of jealousy on her part.

At the outskirts of town, Hamid said, "I hope you'll all be ready to leave for the casino tonight by eight-thirty. If you'll gather in the lobby, I'll have transportation arranged to leave directly from the hotel."

"Aren't you coming along?" Delia wanted to know.

"Not this evening." He was polite but definite. "I have other plans."

"But what if we need any translating?" she protested. "Or do some of the people speak English?"

"Belly dancers get their message across in any language," Herb cut in. "And I hear this one's better than most."

"There's no need to be crude," Delia said.

"Who's being crude?" He sounded amazed. "They tell me this gal at the casino has danced for the biggest diplomatic functions in the country. This kind of dancing is strictly top-drawer over here."

Hamid nodded in confirmation. "Mr. Freeman's right. The casino show is excellent—in the best of taste—and all of the staff speak English. As a special treat, we've planned a typical Moroccan dinner for you before the entertainment. I'm sure you will enjoy it." As he brought the van to a halt in front of their hotel entrance, his glance found Krista's in the rear vision mirror. "Take care, though."

"Take care?" Eve paused in the process of collecting her handbag. "What do you mean by that?"

Hamid was still looking at Krista when he answered lightly. "Merely that you should not eat or drink too much. The food at the casino is excellent, but you're not used to our seasonings."

"Oh, that." Eve was scornful. "We can look after ourselves."

"And you, Mrs. Talbot . . ." Hamid asked insistently. "Do you feel the same way?"

"There's no need for Krista to worry," Jeff cut in as he stepped out of the van. "We'll look out for her. Isn't that right, Ryan?"

Krista didn't wait for any more conversation. She pushed blindly through the bus door and made her way into the hotel.

Ryan caught up with her halfway through the lobby. "What's the hurry?"

She pressed the back of her fingers against her mouth, trying to hide her quivering lips. "I wish you'd let me alone—I was just going up to the room. . . ."

"At a full gallop?"

"Well—I didn't feel sociable."

He shortened his steps but stayed doggedly by her side as they turned into the corridor. "I noticed *that* in the bus. Any use asking what the trouble is this time?"

"I have a headache." Krista pulled up in front of the elevator shaft and jabbed at the button. "But I'd rather not discuss it . . . if you don't mind."

"Not in the least." He stepped aside to let her sweep into the elevator, but then put up a hand to keep the doors from closing. "However, it's time you did a little homework on this venture— once you get over your headache, of course."

She stared at him suspiciously. "What does that mean?"

"Just what I said. Two aspirin and then a written report on your impressions of that zoo. You'd better get them down on paper before you forget anything."

She noted he was back to full employer status in his manner. "If I live to be a hundred," she snapped, "and tied up my notes in red ribbons, I'd remember every part of the afternoon."

He glared back at her. "Do me a favor and spare me from any more cryptic comments. You know it's lucky that you're still in the interesting 'invalid' stage because if you weren't, I'd . . ."

Her eyes narrowed. "You'd what?"

"I'd yank you over my knee, my dear Krista"— he stepped back to let the elevator doors close— "and do a little bruising myself."

Chapter SEVEN

As the evening progressed Krista wished that she could shed the thin veneer of civilization and do something satisfying, like breaking a dinner plate over Ryan's head.

Unfortunately, the staff at the Marrakesh casino wasn't cooperating. For one thing, Ryan was definitely out of reach on their banquette by the stage. For another, he was at the end of the table by Eve's side rather than hers.

It was probably just as well, Krista thought. Since their discussion at the elevator, they had exchanged words that had included only "Excuse me," "Finished with the bath?" and "I'll meet you in the lobby." Not only that, their tones had become more polite and more glacial as time passed and when they finally reached the bus they were exchanging mandarin-like bows with their "After you" and "No, I insist." Jeff had followed the dialogue with a puzzled frown which changed suddenly to an all-knowing grin as they filed into the bus.

Krista came back to the present as she heard a chuckle at her left and turned to find him patiently holding a menu for her.

"Would you like to read what we're going to eat or shall we just drown our sorrows and forget the food entirely?" he asked.

She smiled slightly and took the menu. "I'm

not that desperate yet. Let's see what Moroccans have for dinner."

He shook his head. "Obviously you aren't going to be any help with the drinking side of things. Maybe I'd better ask your husband." He leaned forward over the table. "Ryan—what kind of wine do you drink with cous-cous?"

"That's like asking me what kind of wine I have with pickled sparrows," Ryan said with a chuckle. "I've never had cous-cous before. There's no use asking what Moroccans have with it, either."

"I know." Jeff nodded. "They don't drink hard liquor. But they don't object to selling it to their visitors." He grinned at the hovering waiter. "Isn't that right?"

"Quite right, sir," he responded with a gold-toothed smile. "May I suggest champagne?"

Eve looked up from her perusal of the menu. "I think that's a wonderful idea . . . we'll celebrate—what do you say?"

Jeff looked at the other two for confirmation and then turned back to the waiter. "Champagne it is—something nice. We'll leave it to you."

"I understand, sir. It will be here directly." The waiter gathered their menus and moved away.

Eve watched him go with a pleased look on her face. "I like this place. Who would have thought we'd find such luxury thirty miles from the Sahara?" She gestured to take in the interior of the big round dining room with its filmy gauze draperies on the ceiling and walls. A good-sized stage which doubled as a dance floor occupied the center of the cabaret area where four musicians in black dinner jackets were currently dispensing Western style music. The waiters in their tarbooshes and white djellabahs provided a touch of exotic background and the low damask-covered tables with their upholstered lounges for the patrons heightened the effect.

Jeff squirmed as he tried to fit his six-foot length more comfortably onto the lounge. "I should just lie down like the Romans used to," he complained to Krista. "They had the right ideas about a lot of things."

"Next you'll be wanting me to peel you a grape," she said solemnly, "but don't get carried away—there weren't any on the menu."

He sighed. "Trust a woman to be logical. Besides, I suppose your husband would insist on having exclusive rights to the grape-peeling services."

Ryan overheard him and raised his eyebrows. "That will be the day."

"I make it a point never to go near him with a sharp knife," Krista said sweetly. "It makes him nervous."

"What's all this talk about knives?" Eve asked. "I've read the books and you're supposed to eat cous-cous with your fingers." She frowned down at her elegant black and white print evening dress with its silk taffeta halter. "I hope they furnish bibs."

"Maybe they'll give you a long straw," Jeff suggested. As she frowned, he added hastily, "I was just kidding. Actually, they furnish cutlery if you ask for it."

"Good." She looked between the two men expectantly. "Now, I would like to dance."

Jeff and Ryan exchanged a startled look and then the former hauled a coin out of his pocket and flipped it.

"Heads," Ryan said.

Jeff peered at the brass dirham on his wrist. "I

think it's tails. If a star means tails. It's like flipping a two-headed quarter."

"The music will be over by the time you two finish arguing," Eve complained. "Come on, Ryan . . ." She pulled him up and said over her shoulder to Krista, "You don't mind if I borrow him?" before joining him on the edge of the dance floor.

"There are certain similarities between that young woman and a mechanized panzer division," Jeff pointed out as he watched them merge with the other dancers.

"My husband hasn't noticed."

"On the contrary, it was your husband who pointed it out to me," Jeff said.

Krista was staring at their progress around the dance floor. "He isn't struggling to escape from her stranglehold at the moment."

Jeff started to chuckle. "Now that's more like it," he said finally. "I thought you were going to sit there being a perfect lady for the rest of the night. Shall we dance and give them some competition?"

She smiled but shook her head. "I'd probably trip her if we got near. This way, I can pretend that it doesn't bother me. Thank heavens, we're near the end of the Morocco tour. She isn't going on to Switzerland, is she?"

"Yes . . . but not to Basel. She's scheduled for Geneva and a public health seminar with the Westons and Herb. After that," he said deliberately, "she's flying to Vienna to rejoin her fiancé."

Krista's mouth dropped. "You mean she's engaged?"

He nodded.

"And she still clings like that?" She gestured toward the dance floor.

"Amazing, isn't it? Of course, she could be getting back in practice—or maybe she's just grateful to your husband."

Krista scowled. "Exactly what do you mean by that?"

"Didn't you know? Ryan's the one who advised her how to get her love life back on the track. That's why she kissed him at the zoo this afternoon. You saw that, didn't you?" He watched her lips tighten and grinned before going on. "Yes, I thought you did. Well, that was simply Eve's way of saying 'thank you.' Apparently she'd telephoned her fiancé . . . as instructed . . . and straightened out their misunderstanding. So now the wedding's back on the books after she visits Switzerland, and everything's sweetness and light." He glanced out at the dance floor. "They're coming back to the table. Wonder what happened."

Ryan soon let them know. "Eve wants to rumba and I'm a total loss at it. Jeff—you'd better take over."

Jeff got to his feet and straightened his tie. "Okay, if you say so. But remember, this is a request performance."

"I can't understand why Ryan wouldn't let me teach him—" Eve's voice trailed back as they moved among the dancers. "He just claimed that he could never learn."

Ryan chuckled and then confounded Krista by sitting down in Jeff's place.

She stared across at him, her eyes narrowed to thoughtful slits. "If I remember correctly, you were doing a wicked rumba at Woodsea's Christmas party."

"Ummm." He fished in his pocket for his cigarettes. "You wouldn't have me tell a woman that I didn't want to dance any longer, would you? Between the crowd on the floor and the hammerlock she had on my neck, desperate measures were in order."

Krista's lips started to curve in a smile. "What tactics do you use for me?"

"Don't put words in my mouth," he chided. "Although I must say that it's pleasant to be talking to each other again."

The silence that grew between them was comfortable rather than strained as she watched him light his cigarette and dispose of the match with a neat, decisive movement. Finally, she said, "Jeff told me how you'd helped Eve. He even explained about what happened at the zoo this afternoon."

Ryan frowned at a smoke ring wreathing his head. "I don't know what you're talking about. What *did* happen at the zoo this afternoon?"

"Oh, for heaven's sake ... when she kissed you." As he continued to look blank, she added impatiently, "On the path ... just before you got back to the bus."

"That!" he replied, stung. "You mean that you've been acting like an ice floe because of a simple peck? My God!"

"Well, you could have explained."

"How could I when I didn't even know what you were mad about?" His jaw firmed. "Hell's fire ... I *should* have turned you over my knee."

"I've said I was sorry. . . ."

"When?" There was the beginning of a twinkle in his eyes. "I don't remember it."

"All right then—I'm sorry. But you were a beast to make me write that report."

"I *thought* that would get a response—I should have tried it earlier." He dropped his cigarette in the ashtray and put out a demanding hand. "Come on, let's dance."

"But Eve . . . what will she think?"

"That you persuaded me to try a fox trot," he said, pulling her close to him as they reached the other dancers. When she moved back a discreet distance, he shook her slightly. "Stop behaving like an idiot!"

After that, there was no more conversation— nor any more moving away. Krista couldn't have told how long the medley of show tunes lasted— she was too busy enjoying the harmony of their matching steps, the warmth of Ryan's hand on her back, and the feel of his chin against her hair. When the musicians went into a Latin American encore, Ryan kept her close and executed a neat rumba which won a circle of admirers.

Eve didn't let it pass unnoticed when they returned to the table. "I thought you said you didn't know how to rumba," she accused him as they sat down.

"Was *that* what it was?" He kept his expression solemn. "Krista didn't tell me. I think we'd better change places, Jeff, so I can sit by my wife. She's left-handed, you know, and I'm used to being poked in the ribs when she eats."

Jeff got to his feet, but the grin on his rugged face showed that he saw through the other's subterfuge. "It's nice to know you're both back under the flag again," he said, moving down beside Eve, "but now let's stay put. That's our dinner on the cart and, frankly, I'm starved."

With Ryan by her side, Krista found she thoroughly enjoyed the Moroccan menu that followed. As an appetizer, pungent lamb soup was served in thin porcelain rice bowls. There was a tinge of rosemary in the soup seasoning, adding a piquant flavor to the meat broth which they ate with curved-handled wooden spoons. After the first course was removed, waiters brought in two steaming platters of cous-cous and placed them between the couples. They obligingly brought forks as well when they saw the obvious confusion of their Western visitors.

"Good heavens, there's enough food on that platter to last a growing boy through the winter," Krista said faintly. She leaned forward to inventory the contents. "It looks like a kind of pilaf—rice . . . pieces of lamb. . . ."

"Plus zucchini and onions," Ryan said, peering at his side of the platter. "Aren't those round things *garbanzos?*"

She nodded. "Scads of chick peas and carrot chunks. How do we eat it?"

"Since we're not using our fingers, I suggest transferring a portion to a smaller plate. Then you can spoon some sauce over it. . . ." He watched as she followed his instructions. "Better taste that sauce first . . ." he cautioned as she started to pour it out.

Obediently she dipped into it and felt it scorch as it reached her tongue. "Help! It's their secret weapon!"

Ryan chuckled and pushed the champagne toward her. "I was afraid of that—you'd better cool off with this," he said and leaned over to warn the others.

When the waiter came to remove their plates, he laughed as he saw the untouched bowls of peppery sauce. "Only Moroccans take that," he said proudly. "You need a strong stomach, no?"

"To say nothing of a new mouth," Krista murmured to Ryan before the next course arrived.

"The top of mine feels as if I'd swallowed a flaming sword."

"Maybe this salad will help," he said. "At least it's been chilled."

"Mmmm ... tastes good, too." She took a bite of the sliced oranges sprinkled with coarse sugar and cinnamon. "I definitely think I'll live."

When their glasses of hot mint tea arrived, Jeff sat back and sighed with satisfaction. "All this and dancing girls, too! I should make this place a second home." He glanced up to the stage as he heard a roll of drums, and then consulted his watch. "They're right on time with the floor show."

The regular musicians had left their stand and were being replaced by six men in djellabahs who were carrying drums and strange stringed instruments. As they gathered in a semicircle at the back of the stage, the house lights dimmed and two blue spotlights converged on one of the most beautiful women Krista had ever seen.

She was wearing a pale blue chiffon harem outfit with bouffant trousers and a long-sleeved bare midriff top.

"That costume wasn't whipped up in the souk," Eve murmured.

"Not unless Givenchy has opened a branch in Marrakesh," Krista agreed. "It's gorgeous."

"So's she," Jeff muttered. "Who's looking at her outfit?"

Despite his contention, Krista was sure that at least the feminine portion of the audience was admiring the woman's sense of fashion. The men were undoubtedly noting that the sheer fabric revealed rather than concealed an exquisite full figure with lithe hips and the long thighs so typical of Arab women.

The dancer's dark eyes were outlined by kohl in an exaggerated almond shape but her lustrous dark hair was unadorned and permitted to fall straight to her waist after being pulled back from a narrow forehead. The audience could only guess at the rest of her features because a matching chiffon veil was arranged just below her eyes. Then, as the music increased in tempo, Krista and the rest of the audience forgot about everything except the magnificent sensuality of the dance.

When the drums finally rose to a dramatic crescendo ten minutes later, and the dancer sank gracefully onto the stage directly in front of them, the applause was deafening.

"I'll never say an unkind word about that kind of dancer again," Krista vowed, feeling as if she'd emerged from a hypnotic trance. "She was simply magnificent and the amazing thing was that it was perfectly suitable for all ages. Not an X-rated part in the whole performance."

"You can speak for yourself on that," Jeff said, looking around. "I'd hate to take the blood pressure of some of the men in the audience right now."

Eve was watching the quick background changes being made, "Well, it's going to come down in a hurry, because a snake charmer's next on the program." She shuddered delicately. "I hope they keep the cobras well away from me."

Krista felt the same way as a musician with a reed pipe started a mournful melody and a turbaned individual wearing a white dhoti came out to settle himself on his haunches among the wooden reptile crates.

After the snake charmer, the program continued with a troupe of acrobats who built endless pyramids with enthusiasm but, unfortunately, a limited amount of talent.

As Krista noticed Jeff stifling a yawn, she smiled to herself. Television had taken the edge off such vaudeville acts long ago for most foreign visitors.

"Looks as if the audience is thinning," Ryan commented in an undertone while they were waiting for the next act. "Probably they're heading for the casino next door. Shall we go in and stake a month's salary on roulette?"

"You wouldn't," she exclaimed, horrified.

"Probably not. I don't like to gamble well enough. We could manage a couple of plays, though, without sinking the budget. What do you say?"

"Well, this next group looks like the finale here—" She nodded toward a group of colorfully costumed women filing onto the stage accompanied by male dancing partners who carried two foot-long curved swords. "Maybe we should be polite and wait until they're finished."

"Rather you than me," Eve cut in. "I'd prefer slot machines to native dances. What about you, Jeff?"

He yawned again. "To be honest, I'm on your side. After that first dancer, any others would be an anticlimax. Tell you what," he said to Ryan. "Eve and I will go ahead and save you two a place by the roulette tables. OK?"

"Fine. We'll be along shortly."

It was soon apparent that Moroccan native dances bore a startling similarity to native dances everywhere else in the world.

"After all, they only have four choices . . . backwards, forwards, turn to the left, or turn to the right," Ryan muttered in Krista's ear after they'd watched for another five minutes.

"I know what you mean," she agreed in an undertone. "And, frankly, I wish the men would stop waving those swords so close to us. I thought we were going to be part of a shish kebab on that first chorus. They're too darned enthusiastic for my money."

"Then let's leave when they complete this set. The lights are low enough that nobody will pay any attention."

"What about the bill?"

"It's all taken care of." He folded his napkin on the table as the musicians pounding a set of tom-tom drums thundered to a climax. "Now's the time . . . we'll sneak out during the applause. Give me your hand. . . ."

Krista was close behind him as he stood up and edged toward the exit, so she missed seeing the dancers make their final flamboyant gesture.

No one could have missed, however, the indrawn moan of horror from the audience as the discordant ring of steel clashed behind them. Instinctively both she and Ryan pivoted to see what had happened and their movement was quick enough to see a dancer's sword still quivering in the back of the banquette that they had just vacated.

"My God." Ryan's voice was thick with emotion. "That thing hit just where you were sitting, Krista." As he spoke, the sword pulled loose and fell to the floor with a noisy clatter. A waiter hurried forward to retrieve it and take it away.

"I know." She was staring at the jagged tear in the leather lounge as if hypnotized. Hamid's conversation of the afternoon came back to thud in her memory with each beat of her heart: "I'm warning you now, Mrs. Talbot. You and your husband would do well to leave the country as quickly as possible."

Around them, patrons were settling back in their chairs once they discovered the banquette was unoccupied and that no one had been injured by the flying steel.

Ryan pulled Krista along to the door of the dining room and hesitated under the arch as the music resumed. "Damn it all! Does somebody have to get killed before they cancel the dancing in this place? I'm going to find the man in charge and get some answers out of him."

"Don't, Ryan!" Krista caught his arm before he could move. "It won't do any good."

"The hell it won't. They can at least hire a man for the next show who can hang onto the damned hardware." Now that his initial shock was subsiding, his temper was replacing it. "You wait here . . . or better still I'll take you in with Jeff and Eve. . . ."

"No!" She kept her body deliberately in front of him. "Listen to me, Ryan. You can't get any answers from these people. I should have paid attention to Hamid's warning. We'll simply have to get out of here."

"What's all this about Hamid? I don't understand."

Krista looked around nervously, aware that the diners at the nearby tables were staring at them. "I can't tell you here. Please take me back to the hotel." Her voice was thin and sounded perilously close to the breaking point.

Ryan took one look at her blanched face and caught her around the shoulders as her palms went up to her cheeks.

"Oh, Lord, I feel awful," she whispered against his chest.

"I'll find a cab and get you home. . . ."

She nodded gratefully. "I don't know what's the matter with me . . . I can't imagine why I feel so woozy."

"You're entitled to a first-class case of delayed shock after what's happened." He signaled to the doorman, who took one look at them and hastily motioned for the lead taxi waiting in the rank.

Between the two men, Krista was bundled onto a worn leather seat without further delay.

"Now . . . just stay there for a minute while I leave word for Jeff," Ryan said, straightening. "Will you be all right?"

"Fine . . . now that I'm sitting down," she replied with an attempt at a smile.

"Well, don't try anything else until I get back," he ordered brusquely before turning on his heel and making for the casino entrance again. He had returned before she was able to do more than run a comb through her hair and add some lipstick.

Ryan tipped the doorman and watched him close the door before the driver pulled away in the direction of the hotel. "Jeff and Eve will be along a little later. She'd hit a winning streak on red."

"You didn't say anything . . ."

"About the attempt to skewer us?" His mouth settled in grim lines. "No. How could I? I don't know enough to tell."

Krista replaced the lipstick in her purse and nodded imperceptibly toward the driver. "I'll give you the first installment at the hotel. All right?"

"It'll have to be." Ryan sounded resigned as he settled back on the seat. "I can tell you one thing right now, though—I know I'm not going to like the plot."

A half hour later in their hotel room, he was even more definite in his opinions. "For God's sake, Kris—why didn't you say something about all this before? What happened to your common sense?"

"You're not being fair—what was I to say? Or for that matter what could we have said at the casino tonight? You saw what happened after that sword came crashing down. The dancers simply looked embarrassed and got off the stage as quickly as possible. Nobody suspected that it wasn't an accident, so it wasn't even a case of trying to hush up anything." She rubbed her hand wearily across her forehead and sank down on the edge of the bed. "Hamid knows something about it all—but he's not talking. That's obvious."

"Don't worry. I'll talk to Hamid tomorrow morning." Ryan's tone had a definite edge to it. "That'll be the second thing on my list."

She looked up surprised. "What's first?"

"A couple of airline tickets out of here . . . and that's final," he added as she opened her mouth to protest. "I don't care whether we're in the middle of a political power play or you're harboring an imaginary persecution complex. . . ." He grimaced to take the sting from his words. "I *do* know that the next time you might not be so fortunate. Besides, it only means moving our schedule up a couple of days . . . and the way things are going we can both use a rest period in Switzerland."

"What will you tell Jeff and the others?"

"Jeff will get an outline of the facts in case our State Department's interested. As for the rest of them . . . I'll just say that the heat doesn't agree with you."

"That sounds pretty feeble. . . ."

"Who cares?" He looked disgusted. "If you like, you can pick another excuse before morning, but if you don't get some sleep now, you'll have a ready-made one."

"What's that?"

"An honest-to-God nervous breakdown. You look as if you'd be on the ceiling if there were a backfire from a motor scooter."

"That's ridiculous," she said, getting up and going over to her suitcase for her nightgown. "I'll be perfectly fine after a good night's sleep."

Ryan went over to the dressing table to unload the change from his pockets onto its glass top. "Ummm," he said noncommittally. "We'll see."

Unfortunately, time proved that Ryan was right once again.

By the middle of the night, Krista discovered that the unnerving sword episode, together with the aftereffects of her stairway fall, resulted in a series of dreams and nightmares to rival a terror movie on the late show. After a particularly horrifying episode, she came awake trembling to find Ryan hovering anxiously over her.

"What's the matter, honey?" He cinched the belt on his robe and then sat down on the edge of her bed to smooth her hair from her face. "You were crying out in your sleep."

She rolled her head fretfully on the pillow, still only half awake. "I'm so hot," she murmured, "so hot and thirsty."

"I'll get you a drink. Wait a second until I turn on the bathroom light—then the glare won't get in your eyes."

She felt the mattress spring back as he got up and went over to snap on the light in the bath, leaving the door partially open to provide a subdued light for the bedroom. She moved restlessly, trying to find a cool place on the pillow, and wondered if all nightgowns wound around their victims in a stranglehold or just hers.

Ryan was back before she closed her eyes again. "You'd better sit up," he decided. "Otherwise you'll spill this glass of water again." He helped her push another pillow behind her back as a prop. "That should do it. Now be careful ... this is pretty full. I think we'd better make it a joint effort." He retained his grasp on the glass as she reached for it and, with his free hand, gave her the packet of pills. "It's past time to take a couple more of these."

"They make me feel so woolly," she protested. "Do I have to?"

"You won't get any decent sleep without them. Better follow the doctor's orders."

She nodded resignedly and did as he asked.

"That's the girl." He took the empty glass from her and put it on the table as she sank back and closed her eyes again. The next thing she knew, he was wielding a blessedly cool face cloth over her hot forehead and cheeks.

"Ummm, that feels wonderful."

"An old family prescription." Ryan let the cool cloth linger on her temples and then finished by using the dampened terry on her wrists and hands.

After he had finished, he stood up and said, "You don't look very comfortable. Do you have another nightgown in your bag?"

"Yes ... but you don't need to bother. ..." Her voice trailed off when she found she was addressing his disappearing back.

"You needn't worry about any flaming passions, Kris." His voice was amused as he bent over her suitcase in the hall. "In the first place, it's almost four in the morning, and it's not a habit of mine to take advantage of invalid wives."

"Have you had so many of them?" She was wide awake by then. "Besides, I'm not an invalid."

"You are—for tonight at any rate." He straightened with her spare gown in his hand and moved over to the bathroom door. "I'll even turn off the lights, so we can manage the costume change in the dark. After that," he continued as he snapped the light switch, "you should try for another four hours' sleep. We won't be able to get a plane reservation until later in the day."

Krista felt him sink onto the side of the bed beside her again, the broad width of his shoulders silhouetted against the door of the balcony where moonlight filtered around the curtain.

"Now—raise your arms and let's get you out of that thing," he commanded. "This won't take a minute, honey."

Despite his determinedly impersonal air, they soon discovered that the maneuver had hidden pitfalls. Almost immediately, Ryan's lean fingers came into contact with the soft curve of her breast and he jerked back like a man who had touched a live wire. After that, he let Krista struggle out of the gown alone and when she was getting into the new one, he was careful to avoid any further bodily contact. As a result, by the time Krista was decently covered, he felt like taking a tranquilizer himself. He moved to the safety of his own bed and sighed audibly.

Krista wasn't sure of the reason for his sigh. She only knew that her own nerve ends were screaming in a strange way, which had nothing to do with her physical frailties.

Ryan shrugged out of his robe and then reached for a cigarette from the package on the night table. "I'll take this out on the balcony and smoke it," he said tersely.

"Just in your pajamas? That's a little informal, isn't it?" She tried to match his tone.

"Why not? Who's going to object at four o'clock in the morning? Even the birds are still asleep."

"I don't mind if you smoke it here." She felt a definite reluctance to have him leave the room even though his presence certainly canceled any benefits of her sleeping pill.

"Well, I do. You're supposed to be resting." There was a leashed undertone to his words. "That was the point of this whole damned maneuver. My God, another night like the last two and I'll be old before my time. Now go to sleep or I'll . . ."

"You'll what?"

He started to answer, then shook his head dispairingly and strode to the balcony door, closing it with a muffled crash behind him.

Chapter EIGHT

Their exodus from Morocco the next day may have been a triumph of organization, but it was a definite anticlimax for both of them.

Government officials were magnificently cooperative when they heard the Talbots had to shorten their tour due to Mrs. Talbot's ill health. They would certainly provide transportation to the coast for such distinguished foreign visitors. The trip from Marrakesh to the international airport at Casablanca was tedious at best and Mrs. Talbot would need every comfort. Hamid, they regretted, was not available but there were many English-speaking guides and one would be put at their disposal along with a car. Airline tickets were confirmed by telephone within minutes, and if there were any impending revolutionary activities, they certainly didn't mention them, Ryan said later when he returned to the hotel.

Once the rest of the members of their group heard of the Talbots' leaving, they decided they might as well make their way to the coast with them.

"We'll probably have to wait for a later plane," Jeff said as he and the rest of the group started filing onto their bus shortly after noon, "but it shouldn't take us long. There's lots of air traffic going north and we all make connections for Geneva when we get on the Continent." He let his glance linger on Krista as she settled next to the bus window. "I'm sorry you're not feeling well. Sure you can manage a long plane trip?"

"Of course," she said, trying to look suitably infirm without appearing as a stretcher case. It was too bad that Ryan couldn't have used another excuse for their departure, she decided privately. Unfortunately, the smudges under her eyes and the waxy pallor of her cheeks as a result of her disturbed night gave credence to the story and it was all she could do to keep from yawning outright. Ryan didn't look much better, and after he'd slid onto the seat beside her, he closed his eyes to discourage conversation.

Delia Weston refused to take the hint. "I wonder where Hamid could be?" she asked as their substitute guide slammed the last door and moved around the front of the mini-bus to climb into the driver's seat. "It's a shame not to say good-bye to him after he was so kind to us."

"Write a letter," said her husband. "The Tourist Bureau will know how to get in touch with him."

"I still think it's strange. . . ."

Herb was pulling his visored cap down to shield his eyes from the sun. "Nothing strange about it. Maybe he caught the same kind of bug Krista has. . . ."

"You, of all people, should know that they're not called 'bugs,' " Delia complained.

"Who cares? Frankly, I feel under the weather today, too. I'll be glad to get to Switzerland, where it's a little cooler. This is like the Bronx in August."

"Well, I like it," Eve said, half turning in the seat to smile at Ryan's lanky figure. "I'll always have fond memories of this place, although"—her smile became dreamy—"I'm anxious to be moving on."

"That's easy to understand. I hear congratulations are in order for you." Delia's tone was arch. "Have you set a date yet?"

Eve shook her head. "I'm flying on to meet Kurt in Vienna after my conference in Geneva. We'll decide about the wedding then."

"Well, at this rate, we'll have to schedule our farewell drink in Casablanca," Jeff said. "It'll be hard to go back to work after a week off."

"Some of us," Delia told him pointedly, "have been working even in Morocco."

He refused to take offense. "Then you deserve two drinks at the airport. Such virtue must be rewarded."

Their driver increased his speed once they left Marrakesh, and Krista felt her eyelids droop. When the van stopped a little later, she found that she was propped against Ryan's shoulder. Drowsily, she stared out through the bus window at the endless fields of corn and wheat surrounding them, and wondered whether she should sit up and take an interest in things. Then Ryan's arm tightened around her and she was settled more comfortably in the hollow of his shoulder. She smiled gratefully and let her eyes close again.

This Rip Van Winkle state of affairs lasted for the whole trip to Casablanca. It was considerably later—after they'd boarded their jet—before she could stay awake long enough to comment on it. "I don't know what's the matter with me," she apologized to Ryan, sitting in the aisle seat beside her. "There must have been a sleeping pill in the breakfast coffee or that drink Jeff bought."

Ryan smiled and bent over to check her seat belt as their jet taxied down the runway. "Jeff's merely in the State Department ... not some hush-hush branch of the C.I.A. You're imagining things again."

"I know"—Krista was trying to keep her mind from the whine of the jet engines as they were tested at the end of the runway—"but he must be more important than we thought."

"What gives you that idea?" Ryan reached across to take her hand in a comforting grip.

"Well ..." She forgot to finish her sentence and clung to his fingers tightly as the big jet started on its takeoff. Then suddenly they were up in clear blue Moroccan skies and the rich coastal farmlands were a gigantic checkerboard beneath them. Krista's grip relaxed, but Ryan kept his hand over hers. "Well," she managed to say again, "I woke up two times on the way to Casablanca—when we were stopped at the roadblocks. After the officials looked at Jeff's credentials, we were just waved politely through. They were being a lot more thorough with the rest of the traffic on the road."

"We were V.I.P.s. You're not used to the visiting dignitary role." As the *No Smoking* signs clicked off above them, he reached in his coat pocket for his cigarettes. "Anyway, if you're really curious, you can ask Jeff in person. He plans to drop in on our seminar in Basel later this week."

"Official business?"

"Just partly." Ryan grinned. "Strictly off the record, he needed an excuse to visit the zoo there. Wants to see their *Affenhaus* . . . ape house to you," he teased.

"You needn't translate," she said loftily. "What's so great about it?"

"It's brand-new construction. Magnificent combination of indoor and outdoor cages with three viewing levels to accommodate all ages. When you add a great collection of primates, you have a zoo director's dream."

"Well, you can look at their *Affenhaus* and I'll look at the pygmy goats. We need some in Woodsea's nursery. Think how the children would love them."

"To say nothing of the nursery director."

She smiled at his teasing. Then her expression became thoughtful. "I wonder when Hamid's friend will get in touch with us. It's too bad we couldn't make arrangements before we left. This way it's so indefinite." She was peering through the plane window as the jet continued to climb. "Look how clear it is out there—there isn't a bit of cloud cover."

Ryan ignored her last comment. "Who's Hamid's friend and what does he have to do with us?" He frowned suddenly at her guilty look. "You mean there's more you haven't told me?"

Her hand went up to her mouth. "I guess I forgot. Honestly, Ryan, it didn't have anything to do with the other." She hastily repeated Hamid's request at the zoo, and at the end of her recital, she rummaged in her purse. "I wrote his name down afterward so I could remember. . . . Here it is! Abdellatif Amid Khaoulan."

"And he's supposed to be a red-hot Arabic translator?"

"That's what Hamid said."

Ryan rubbed the bridge of his nose thoughtfully. "Do you have that book handy . . . the one Hamid gave you?"

"Uh-huh." She delved in her big purse again. "It's still in here . . . I keep forgetting to put it in my suitcase or the basket."

He took it from her and leafed through the

thin pages slowly. "Too bad Luther isn't on this plane." At her puzzled look, he explained: "Jeff told me that the Westons know some Arabic. Even a little would help confirm Hamid's story about this. . . ." He closed the book and weighed it deliberately in his hand.

"I wonder if you're not imagining things now."

"Maybe—but why bring in this Abdellatif fellow for translating?"

"Hamid explained that the man's a zoo buff. Perhaps he wants to come and visit Woodsea sometime. You know how it helps to have some personal contacts if you're traveling." She was watching the stewardess start down the aisle taking orders for cocktails. "I hope they serve dinner pretty soon. Frankly, I'm starved."

"So am I. Well, I suppose we'll learn the answers to all this confusion sometime." Ryan handed back the book and watched her stuff it into her purse. "If Hamid's friend doesn't show in Basel, maybe we can eventually ask the Westons."

"It was strange how they wanted to meet us again in Basel after their Geneva seminar. Even Eve and Herb sounded tempted."

"They were all interested in that zoo in Marrakesh as well," Ryan mused, "and it wasn't great. Either they're animal lovers or just crazy about our personalities."

"If you're talking about Eve . . ."

"I'm not," he said firmly. "We've settled that discussion once and for all."

The afternoon lengthened and the drone of the jet engines continued steadily as they climbed above the clouds covering the Mediterranean. Life aloft became a succession of cocktails, dinner, soft drinks, snacks (airline parlance for finger sandwiches), and then dinner again. By the time they emerged from the landing pattern at Rome's busy airport, Krista felt a kinship with Phineas Fogg and his hot air balloon. "What now? Bed?" Her tone was hopeful as they struggled off the plane.

Ryan shook his head. "Sorry, honey. Customs first—then we still have a long way to go. There's a pretty good connection to Milan in an hour."

The Milan connection was delayed, so it was considerably later when they struggled down the next set of airplane steps.

"I'm afraid to ask," Krista murmured, wishing she could curl up as a sensible French poodle was doing while his owner waited for some luggage. "What idiot said that distances were nothing in Europe?"

Ryan yawned. "I don't know ... but he obviously wasn't coming from North Africa." He moved into the luggage line behind the poodle's owner. "We'd better have some breakfast ... or maybe it's lunch."

Krista was eyeing a coffee bar nearby. "Some coffee would help, but I can't face another hard roll. Are you sure you don't need to visit Italian zoos? I'd wait at a hotel. . . ."

"How about a nice Swiss zoo instead? You can sleep on the train."

"Well, I've slept on everything else. How did we happen to miss a camel or ox cart when we left Marrakesh?"

He grinned. "Couldn't get reservations on them." As their bags came into view, he said, "Go order a couple of cappuccinos—the caffeine should keep us awake until we get to the railroad station."

The Italian train was fine, Krista discovered, except that their compartment was full of Italians ... happy, well-fed Italians who took up their seats and overflowed onto the adjoining ones. It was impossible for her or Ryan to do other than sit erect and watch the green countryside through eyes glazed with weariness. When they reached the Swiss border, a steward came through their car announcing another meal.

"I can't," Krista said flatly. "They served salami in hard rolls just a half hour ago. Besides, it's fifteen cars back to the diner."

"Fourteen." Ryan rubbed his neck. "I counted them."

"It doesn't matter. This train's longer than a Southern Pacific freight. By the time we got to the diner, we'd be halfway back to Milan. Maybe if we walked forward to the engine, we'd be in Basel . . ." she added hopefully.

"Lucerne." Ryan moved his head on the velour seat and tried to ignore the interested glances of the four other people in their compartment. "This train goes to Lucerne . . . we have one more transfer to Basel. It's an hour or so beyond."

"Did you ever see that movie called *Murder on a Train?*"

"No."

"Stick around."

He leaned forward uneasily. "I'm sorry, Kris. You must be half-dead by now. Tell you what . . . we'll stay overnight in Lucerne. We can call our hotel in Basel and say we've been delayed. That way, we can sleep late in the morning. . . ."

"Stop right there," she told him. "I'm not making any plans beyond that."

"Fair enough. Now, keep your fingers crossed for a vacant hotel room when we arrive in Lucerne."

It was almost ten-thirty that night when the train finally pulled into the popular Swiss resort city. The porter who materialized for their luggage obligingly directed them to the hotel reservation kiosk in the station.

"Go along quickly," he said in excellent, though strangely accented English. "The reservation desk closes shortly and hotel rooms are very difficult to find. I'll have your bags waiting by the taxi stand at the station entrance."

Ryan set off with his long strides and Krista had to hurry to keep up with him. They arrived at the glass-fronted tourist booth just as a gray-haired woman was putting on her coat, but she smiled and dropped it on a chair as Ryan asked for her help.

After he'd finished, she pursed her lips and shook her head doubtfully. "It's so late—I doubt if there's anything left tonight, unless there's a cancellation."

Krista sighed audibly. "Maybe we'll have to go back to the United States to find a place to sleep."

Ryan leaned persuasively on the reservation counter. "If you could phone some of the hotels," he said, using his most engaging manner with the older woman, "we'd be very grateful."

She turned slightly pink under his look and picked up the phone. "I *do* have a friend who works at our nicest hotel and there's always a chance ..." She broke off to conduct her telephone conversation in a spate of Schweizer-Deutsch with the unknown friend. Finally she hung up and turned to them, beaming. "You *are* in luck. They have one room left—and it's a nice one overlooking the lake. Take this address"—she was writing on a slip of paper as she spoke—"and give it to your taxi driver. Don't waste any time—there's not another thing left in town."

Ryan took the paper. "You've been very kind. I don't know how to thank you."

"Just enjoy your stay in Switzerland." She made a shooing motion with her hands. "But go along now . . . that's positively the only hotel room in Lucerne tonight."

Ten minutes later, the hotel desk clerk was repeating her words. "You are fortunate to find this cancellation. I'll call your hotel in Basel to say your arrival will be delayed." He smiled as he added, "Hotel space is at a premium there as well . . . so they will be glad to have the extra accommodation. Now . . . my colleague will take you to your room and the porter will bring your luggage along later. I hope you sleep well."

Krista yawned twice as they waited for the elevator. She could have told the desk clerk that he didn't need to worry—after thirty-six straight hours of traveling it was doubtful whether she or Ryan could even stay awake long enough to brush their teeth.

It only took the opening of their hotel room door to make her realize how wrong she was.

The two of them exchanged one startled glance before silently following their host into the high-ceilinged room with its vast adjoining bathroom. They stared obediently as he pointed out the huge armoires, the two balcony windows overlooking the lake, and the tempting basket of fruit provided by the hotel management.

They waited until he'd left the key and ceremoniously bowed himself out before their gaze went fixedly back to the brass double bed occupying the exact center of the room.

Then Ryan slumped against an armoire and shoved his hands into his pockets. His glance moved from the bed to Krista, where she stood motionless by the desk. "What the hell do we do now?" he asked finally.

She bit her lip as she put her purse on the desk blotter. "I suppose there's no use asking about another room . . .?"

"You heard the desk clerk—*and* the woman at the station."

She nodded with resignation and then uttered a breathless laugh as thunder rumbled in the distance. "A storm, too. Hardly a night for us to walk the streets." She started to shrug out of her topcoat. "Well, we might as well make the best of it. After all, there's no reason why we can't act like two adults for one night. We're exhausted . . . it's a big bed and we can trust each other not to . . ."

"No." Ryan's tone was flat but definite.

"I beg your pardon. . . ."

"I said no." He stared impassively at her without moving from his place. "You can forget that angle."

"I . . . I don't know what you mean."

"Oh, for God's sake, Krista—do I have to spell it out?" He moved slowly toward her, sounding like a man who'd reached the end of his tether and didn't care who knew it. "No more nice platonic nights. Not if we share that bed. That's final."

She swallowed and took a backward step, feeling her tiredness melt away like snow under a springtime sun. Then she realized she was against the edge of the desk and couldn't retreat any farther.

He reached out and yanked her numbed figure against his. "We have a perfectly good marriage certificate and I'm damned tired of playing games. If I stay, there'll be a good deal of this"—he bent over and kissed her hard while his hands moved deliberately, caressingly, down from her shoulders to her hips—"and probably a hell of a lot more. Other than that, I'm not promising a thing," he added roughly when he finally raised his head from her parted lips. "Now, what's it to be? Do I go or stay?"

Krista stared dazedly up at him. Where had she got the idea that Ryan didn't know how to handle women? Even his glance was enough to make her bones turn to clay, and his possessive hands were arousing a desire she'd never felt before. She tried to ignore the tears that were filling her eyes as he waited for an answer. Thunder rumbled through the sky again but it was scarcely evident over the pounding of her heartbeat.

Ryan's jaw tightened as he saw the indecision in her face and his hands fell to his sides. "I didn't think it would be so hard for you to make up your mind. Evidently you haven't spent the last week losing sleep the way I did."

"Honestly, I didn't realize . . . I had no idea." She faltered, wondering why the man couldn't make it easier for her. No woman wanted to bare her soul this way. If he'd just tell her he loved her as much as she loved _him_ . . . then they'd solve everything.

Krista drew in her breath sharply as her thoughts crystallized. Of course she loved him—she had all along. Being in his arms . . . feeling his lips on hers was sheer heaven. She couldn't send him away. Not now. Not tonight. Surely every woman was entitled to spend one night with the man she adored.

Ryan must have read her thoughts because his eyes darkened and he reached over to pull her yielding body against his. "Say it, Kris. Shall I stay or go?"

From the tone of his voice, from the way his glance lingered on her lips, she knew it was too late for escape. Deliberately, she slipped her arms around his neck and drew his head down again. Even then he could hardly hear her whispered "Don't go, Ryan darling, please don't go."

It was the middle of the night when the center of the storm advanced over the lake and wakened them with thunder crescendos and brilliant spider webs of heat lightning.

Ryan must have heard Krista's quickened breathing as a stab of lightning illuminated their windows because his arm immediately tensed and tightened across her waist. Moments later, she felt the caressing, insistent movements of his hands and mouth.

A delicious warmth stole over her until their lips met in a hard and seeking kiss. Then her response was unchecked and passion flared like a vital thing between them as she surrendered eagerly to his demands once again.

Later, she noticed the diminishing rumble of thunder as she was drowsing off to sleep. She smiled and settled more comfortably against Ryan's side—aware that the tempest outside was nothing compared to the one which had raged between them.

Chapter *NINE*

The melodious clamor of church bells awakened Krista the next morning. For a moment she lay quietly, enjoying the measured and resonant melodies which echoed from the steep mountain slopes surrounding the lake.

Then the memory of the previous night's happenings engulfed her thoughts and she pushed up an elbow to stare at the bed beside her.

It was empty.

Her puzzled glance moved swiftly around the semidarkened room. It was empty, too. Only the soft morning breeze moved the rose taffeta curtains at a balcony window pushed partially ajar. A thin ribbon of sunlight filtered along the curtain edges to bathe the ivory carpet in a rosy glow.

Krista's heartbeat speeded up with alarm and then steadied as she observed a small breakfast tray on the desk. She started to smile when she noted the crumpled napkin and carelessly folded newspaper which had been tossed on top of it. Evidently Ryan had breakfasted earlier and then left the room so that she could catch up with her sleep.

Her cheeks warmed at the necessity for such a maneuver. Ryan was displaying all sorts of unexpected and endearing qualities, she decided. For a moment, she lay back on the pillow and allowed herself to dream on them before reluctantly throwing back the covers and putting her feet on the floor. If she hurried with her shower she could be dressed and ready to leave by the time Ryan returned. That way there wouldn't be any delay if he wanted to go on to the zoo. Or did people visit zoos on honeymoons? Maybe he'd have another plan in mind after last night.

She stood irresolute for a second by the side of the bed. Then she grinned impishly as she headed for the bathroom. Maybe "people" didn't ... but Ryan would. Husband or not, he hadn't changed *that* much.

There was a knock on the outer door as Krista reached the hall. Before she could answer it, the knob turned and an elderly maid stuck her head cautiously around the jamb.

"*Morgan*, Frau Talbot." She switched laboriously into thick English. "I came to pick up the breakfast tray. All right?"

"Of course." Krista waved her into the room. "Could I order some coffee and rolls, please?"

"*Ja ... ja ...*" The maid started to refold the newspaper and then briskly tucked it under her arm before picking up the tray. "When would you like your breakfast?"

"About fifteen minutes from now will be fine." Krista hovered in the archway and wondered about ordering more coffee for Ryan's return. Then, as the maid looked at her questioningly, she compromised with: "Plenty of coffee, please—and would you bring honey instead of jam for the rolls?"

The woman nodded. "Hot milk or cream for your coffee, *bitte?*"

"Cream, thanks," Krista said, happy that the menu was beginning to sound a little like home.

"Danke," the other replied as Krista began to close the door behind her. "Fifteen minutes."

Krista was just applying the last touch of cologne at the bathroom mirror when she heard the rattle of dishes in the hall and looked at her watch. Fifteen minutes exactly. No wonder the Swiss were acclaimed as hotelkeepers. She took a final glance at her long-sleeved beige blouse which looked tailored and sleek above her beige and rust herringbone skirt. After a week in Morocco, it was nice to put away her cotton clothes. Woolens were more in keeping with the fresh breeze from Lake Lucerne. An earlier glimpse through the window showed snow still covering the mountain peaks and there was a tang to the air which even the sunlight couldn't dispel.

Krista stepped out into the bedroom and found a smiling waiter carefully arranging her breakfast things.

"Good morning, Mrs. Talbot. I hope you find everything as you like it." His gesture took in a silver coffeepot, the plate of fresh rolls with foil-wrapped butter, and a brand-new copy of the international *Herald Tribune* folded by her plate.

"It looks wonderful, thank you." She sat down in the chair he was holding and unfolded her napkin. "I'd better hurry or it will be lunchtime."

He smiled and smoothed the front of his immaculate starched coat. "There is plenty of time. Mr. Talbot told us that you weren't to be disturbed."

Krista's head shot up. "You saw my husband? This morning?"

"Of course." He reached over to pour her coffee. "I delivered Mr. Talbot's breakfast earlier. Then, when he went out, I directed him to the side entrance so he could meet the young woman in her car. They drove off"—he consulted his watch carefully—"about three hours ago."

"The young woman in her car," Krista said, dazed.

"I beg your pardon. . . ."

She made an effort to pull herself together. "Did Mr. Talbot happen to say when he was coming back?"

The waiter's eyebrows climbed. Obviously Swiss wives didn't ask questions like that. "No, madam. Mr. Talbot merely thanked me for directing him." He edged toward the door. "If there's nothing else . . ."

Krista fumbled for the newspaper and buried her head in it, so he wouldn't see the unshed tears in her eyes. "Nothing, thank you."

"Then just ring for the maid when you are finished. Enjoy your breakfast, *bitte.*"

She waited until the door had closed behind him before she dropped the newspaper and stood up, moving over to the open balcony window. Breakfast was forgotten as she stared along the lakefront while her mind tried to assimilate the waiter's words.

Why on earth had Ryan stolen out of the hotel at dawn without waking her or at least leaving a message? More to the point—who was the young woman in the car who had accompanied him?

Krista's features grew stormy as she thought about it. Surely a man should tell his wife a few basic facts, so that she wouldn't worry. He owed her that much. Especially after a night when he'd promised . . .

She frowned as she tried to remember exactly what he'd promised.

Nothing really.

She hadn't thought to question him then—to

analyze his motives—to wonder if he'd felt as she did. There had only been time to marvel ... to feel his sense of urgency as her own ... and finally to glory in the fulfillment of their love.

Now she was discovering that an evening's indiscretion didn't necessarily mean a lifetime commitment for a man, and that the cold morning light contained shadows as well as sunshine.

That left only one thing for her to do.

She turned blindly back into the bedroom and dragged her suitcase onto the bed. If Ryan thought she was going to trail him around Europe so that he could make love to her whenever he found time ... he was sadly mistaken.

If only she'd made her resolutions before she'd thrown herself into his arms last night, she wouldn't be in this predicament now. Or if she'd thought to notice that there were never any promises of eternal love and affection. That was strictly wishful thinking on her part.

A tear dripped onto the slip she was packing and she dried her cheeks impatiently. Without wasting any more time, she retrieved her cosmetic bag from the bathroom and threw it into the suitcase with more force than was necessary.

Then she marched over to the closet to pull out her rust suede topper. After putting it on and belting it tightly, she closed the suitcase and set it by the door.

She went back to the bedroom to see if she'd forgotten anything, and caught sight of the bulging basket that Ryan had bought for her in Tangier. Tears welled in her eyes again as she stared down at its familiar outlines. Then her expression grew bleak—for two cents she'd leave it with him to show how little his presents meant. She walked over and fingered the silly whisk broom protruding from the handles. Then, almost reluctantly, she picked up the basket and moved it over beside her suitcase. It wasn't much of a souvenir for one week of marriage, but at least it was something to offset her unhappy memories which were bound to linger for a lifetime.

When she reached the lobby, she made her way to the concierge's cubbyhole by the reception desk. "Would you send up to 211 for my bags, please," she said, trying to sound brisk and matter-of-fact. "Then I'd like a taxi to the station."

"Room 211? If you wish, madam." He hesitated and leaned on the counter as he noted her agitation. "Could I help you with anything?"

"I'm not sure." She noted thankfully that his English was as polished as the brass buttons on his uniform. "Would you know the quickest way to leave the country?"

His leathery face cracked in a smile. "East? West? Or straight up? We Swiss can even arrange for that."

Krista managed to respond with a faint smile. "That did sound desperate, didn't it? Actually, I've just heard that I have to get home in a hurry. Where could I get the best connections for a flight to the States?"

His face sobered immediately. "I should think Paris or Rome. You're Mrs. Talbot, aren't you?" He waited for her nod and went on. "Normally you could connect in Zurich, but there are so many tourists in Switzerland now that reservations are almost impossible. You would do better to take a train to France or Italy and get a direct flight to the States from there."

"I see." She chewed on her thumbnail and tried to think logically. "Italy would be easier, I guess. When is the next train to Rome?"

He reached for a thick book of schedules. "We have many trains but you'll want a Trans-European Express. There are two daily ... the best one leaves Lucerne at five o'clock this afternoon."

"Not until then!" Her face fell. She couldn't wait in the hotel lobby for another four hours and take a chance on having Ryan see her when he returned. From now on, any confrontations would be between their lawyers. This last resolve was so drastic that her eyes suddenly welled with tears again.

The concierge didn't know what caused them but a vast experience with women prompted him to say helpfully, "There's no need to worry, Mrs. Talbot. I will arrange for your rail tickets and call the airline as well. You can leave your luggage here until you come back this afternoon." He reached for his pencil. "Both you and your husband will be going?"

"Oh, no. The tickets are just for me."

"I see." The two words contained a wealth of understanding. "Very well, Mrs. Talbot. If you'll be back here by half-past three, everything should be well in hand." As she hesitated, he added in kindly fashion, "There's an interesting excursion you could take in the meantime if you want to see some of the countryside."

"That sounds like a good idea."

"I have a booklet here that describes it." His expression was concerned as he searched under the counter. It would be a shame if Mr. Talbot didn't get back to the hotel before the Rome train. It would be still a bigger shame if Mrs. Talbot ever found out there was a perfectly good Rome express leaving Lucerne in forty minutes. He opened the sightseeing booklet briskly and began to read. "No visit to Lucerne is complete without a tour to the summit of Pilatus. Like the Eiffel Tower in Paris . . . Big Ben in London . . ."

"And Grant's Tomb in New York," she cut in. "I understand. But where is this Mount Pilatus?"

He looked wounded. "Directly across the lake, Mrs. Talbot. All seven thousand feet of it. The storm last night centered around it."

Krista didn't choose to linger on last night's storm and its consequences. "Is there a sightseeing trip leaving fairly soon? After all, I can't risk too much time if I get my train. . . ."

This time he cut *her* off. "The launch leaves in five minutes from the Nationalquai directly in front of this hotel. Just take this ticket and give it to your guide. . . ."

"Well, if you think it's all right . . ." she began.

He came around the counter and took her by the elbow. "I do, Mrs. Talbot. Most assuredly. Go right through our main entrance, down the front steps, and across the promenade. You will see the launch at the pier."

She made one last stand. "You'll take care of my luggage. . . ."

"Of course. Now, don't worry, Mrs. Talbot. Enjoy Pilatus . . ." he beamed. "On such a day, the view from the summit should be magnificent. Have a good trip." He watched her go down the hotel steps and gave her a farewell wave before she disappeared beyond the chestnut trees bordering the lakeside walk. Then he allowed himself a sigh of relief, deciding he was too old for a marriage counselor's role.

As he walked back to his office, his attention was caught by a bellboy carrying a slate with Mrs. Talbot's name scrawled upon it. The concierge's eyes grew thoughtful—then definitely amused as he reached for the telephone receiver on his counter.

Krista found the motor launch without difficulty and let a husky crewman swing her on deck before he went forward to loosen the bowline.

A thin gray-haired woman with a pleasant smile met her at the glass-covered cabin amidships. "That was cutting it close. Welcome to the Pilatus excursion . . . I'm Trina, your guide." She was taking Krista's ticket as she spoke.

"I didn't have time to read the booklet," Krista began, "so I don't know anything about it."

"That doesn't matter . . . I'll explain as we go along. Right now you can enjoy the lake scenery as we cross over to the Pilatus railway on the opposite side." Trina smiled and indicated an empty seat in the crowded cabin.

The hostess watched Krista take her place and picked up a microphone by the front of the cabin. "Now, ladies and gentlemen, in approximately twenty minutes, we will dock at Alpnachstad near the base of our famous mountain. There we will board a very old and famous cogwheel railway going directly to the summit of the peak. This railway is also one of the steepest constructed with a maximum gradient of forty-eight percent." She waited for a murmur of appreciation to subside before going on briskly. "It takes approximately one half hour to go from Alpnachstad to the summit of Pilatus, with breathtaking scenery all the way. Imagine, ladies and gentlemen . . . we will be ascending over one mile in one half hour."

Krista blinked with amazement. The concierge hadn't been far wrong when he said Swiss visitors could go straight up.

"At the summit of the mountain, you will find

two famous hotels for tourists who want an overnight stay. Of course, our visit will be much shorter." She paused for a professional smile. "Just long enough for you to enjoy a cup of coffee or purchase our famous Swiss chocolate. On our return journey down the other side of the mountain, we will descend on a large aerial cable car first—suspended from steel cables for a breathtaking six-minute plunge in space. . . ."

Krista swallowed. What in the world had she stumbled into? Next time, she'd make sure that she read the darned booklet first. . . .

"This type of cableway was used in a recent James Bond film where the actors fought outside on the car roof as it descended over the mountain chasms," Trina was explaining with a coy smile. "We won't expect you to imitate them—in fact, we'll make sure you're all locked in so you won't be tempted."

The woman next to Krista sniffed disdainfully and turned to her husband. "Very funny," she muttered. "What does she think we are—a bunch of idiots?"

Trina pretended not to hear. "After the cableway," she said, "we board another cable car at Frakmuntegg. These cabins hold four persons . . . similar to your ski lifts in the States. From there, we descend to lake level near Lucerne in approximately twenty minutes. Now—are there any questions?"

"Yeah," growled a masculine voice from the last row of seats. "Where do we get our money back?"

Trina laughed with the rest. "Believe me, you'll always remember your afternoon on the mountain. It should be especially memorable today as the cloud cover at the summit is disappearing.

That's a good sign. Our people say that the spirit of Pontius Pilate haunts the summit and causes dreadful storms if too many people disturb him. But if he's resting and it's clear, I'll point out the Jura Mountains as well as the Black Forest to the north. You'll get your first glimpse of them on the cog railway as we go up."

Later, when Krista slid onto the wooden seat of the rail car and looked around her, she had a sneaky suspicion of what was to come. The car was constructed so that each row was considerably higher than the one in front of it, like a steep football stadium. When the doors were securely locked by the security guards and the car started its ascent of the mountainside, each person was afforded an unobstructed view of the panorama unfolding beneath them.

"Notice the magnificent views of Lucerne and the entire Lake of the Four Cantons," Trina trilled from the back seat.

Krista managed one look over the alpine countryside and felt her stomach turn over in horror. For a person who didn't even like express elevators, the cogwheel train which went up the sheer rock face like a mountain goat was an utter nightmare. Why, thought Krista miserably as she sat with lowered eyes, why didn't they furnish parachutes? Or stairways for emergency exits?

The train edged steadily upward, past protruding rock slopes and through alpine meadows where snow patches still lingered between the wildflowers. There were a few curious brown cattle in the steep lower pastures but they were the only living souls on the long journey.

When they finally jerked onto the landing platform at the towering Pilatus summit thirty minutes later, Kris couldn't crawl out of the bright red car fast enough. She sighed with profound relief as she stepped on solid ground once again, following the others through the landing tunnel into the brilliant sunshine.

A long cemented platform built to cover the razor-sharp summit ridge served as a place to take pictures of the magnificent scenery stretched out below them. Most of the tour group were already unpacking their cameras as they headed for it.

"Don't forget, ladies and gentlemen," Trina called after them. "We will board the aerial cable car in approximately twenty minutes. You'll find me at Platform B. Remember now—just twenty minutes."

Krista decided that solitude was called for while she got over the effects of the cogwheel railway and girded herself for the impending cable descent. She wandered along the walk, carefully staying out of range of the photographers and skirting a Spanish tour group which was huddled in a patch of sunshine near the entrance to one of the hotels. Now that she was at the summit, she felt no inclination to hang over the railings as so many of the visitors were doing. The vast expanse of Alpine grandeur made her feel more lonely than ever, and the glimpses of tiny huts clinging in the valleys far below simply made her wish that she was in the American Rockies and not thousands of miles from home. She strolled on down to the isolated end of the walk and stared at a rocky finger where vegetation was struggling to grow after the severe Swiss winter.

"You don't look as if you care for the scenery, Mrs. Talbot," said a soft masculine voice behind her.

She jerked around, startled, to see Hamid leaning negligently against the railing a few feet away. He moved over beside her as she stared.

"I didn't mean to startle you," he apologized. "Actually I came up on the same car but you evidently didn't see me."

A faint smile came to her lips. "After the first three minutes, I had my eyes closed most of the way. I can't stand heights," she confessed. "This is a pretty silly place for me to be, isn't it?" She watched him smile in sympathy. In a well-cut trench coat with a turned-up collar and wearing a black beret on the side of his head, he presented a far different appearance than the guide who'd met them in Tangier. "We were sorry not to say good-bye to you in Marrakesh," she went on pleasantly as he simply stood there. "This must have been an unexpected trip for you. Did you come to visit your friend?"

His black eyebrows drew together. "What friend is that?"

"Why . . . the one in Basel that you told me about. The one with the long name who could translate my book."

Hamid's expression relaxed. "Oh, Abdell . . . possibly we'll meet later." He edged closer and Krista would have retreated instinctively if she hadn't felt the low stone barrier cut into her back. "I wanted to talk to you about that book . . . Mrs. Talbot. Did you bring it with you?"

Her hand went to her purse and then dropped again to her side. "Yes, I have it. Why?"

"I found that I had left some personal memos in it by mistake." His tone was low-pitched, confidential, but his eyes didn't leave her face for an instant. "I want it back, Mrs. Talbot." As she started to frown, he went on in the same implacable monotone. "I mean to *have* it back, Mrs. Talbot."

She managed a weak defense. "And if I don't agree . . ."

"That would be very silly." He looked over his shoulder before turning back to her. "There isn't anyone paying the slightest attention to us. When people are careless up here—accidents can happen." He bent down to pick up a pebble and flick it over the barrier disdainfully.

Krista watched it skitter down the vertical rock face and disappear in an instant's time. She turned a white, horrified face back to him.

He was still glancing after it with a strange smile on his lips. "A person would be five hundred feet down before he bounced the first time. . . ."

"You wouldn't dare . . ." She broke off as his cruel gaze swept over her then like honed steel.

"Don't be a fool!" he snapped. "Who do you suppose arranged the mishap in Fez—the near-accident in Marrakesh . . .?"

"But why? What was the point of it?" Her eyes were still wide with disbelief.

"That's none of your affair. Give me that purse. . . ." He stuck out an imperative hand. "The book is in it?"

Krista tried to think as she slid the strap from her shoulder reluctantly. "I guess it is. Honestly, I can't remember. . . ."

Hamid paid no attention. He unzipped the top with a ruthless gesture and was rifling the contents even as she protested. Finally, he looked up, his face livid with fury. "It isn't there. What have you done with it? Tell me, you little . . ."

Krista felt his fingers clamp onto her forearm with a grip that made her whimper with pain.

"Where is it?" he snarled again, waving the open bag under her face.

"Honestly . . . I don't know. It was there the last time I looked. Unless Ryan . . ." Her voice trailed off as his grip tightened.

"Unless Ryan what?"

She tried to free her wrist and merely succeeded in making him twist it again. "I'm *trying* to tell you," she gasped. "Maybe he took it with him. He was going into Basel today and he knew about your friend."

He dropped her arm with a stifled oath. For a second he just stood there—his eyes flashing angrily. Then his gaze moved over the low railing where he'd flung the stone onto the jagged cliffs below. He was obviously trying to decide whether she'd be a help or a hindrance in his future moves.

"I'm going to meet Ryan at the hotel after the tour," she put in desperately, hoping to divert his thoughts. "He's sure to be back by now. He'll have the book with him. I could get it for you. . . ."

They were interrupted by the shrill blast of a whistle and looked down the walk to see Trina beckoning imperiously at Krista. "Come along, please!"

"What is this?" Hamid muttered, putting a restraining hand on her shoulder. "What does that infernal woman want?"

"We just had twenty minutes here," Krista babbled, almost incoherent in her relief. No man could be desperate enough to shove a victim over a railing with an irate Swiss tour guide looking on. "She wants us to get on the cable car for the return. . . ."

"Very well." He thrust her back along the walkway. "You can keep the appointment. Only this time, I'll be right beside you. We'll go to the hotel and see your husband in person." He was marching her along smartly as he spoke. "Don't get any stupid thoughts about calling for help . . . my whole future depends on that book. I'd go to any lengths to retrieve it." From his implacable tone, Krista had no doubt that he meant every word.

"And in case you're even tempted," he went on more softly as they caught up with the stragglers on the tour, "I have a knife." He felt her shudder and gave a mirthless grin. "This time you wouldn't have such a lucky escape, believe me."

"*There* you are!" Trina was hailing her from the chain barrier by the entrance to a tunnel opposite the cog railway landing. "You must come along . . . we have a schedule to keep. Only forty people are allowed on this tram and our tour members are given priority. You've kept all the others waiting," she scolded briskly. Then, as she eyed Hamid with suspicion, "This man isn't part of our group."

Krista felt a sharp prick in her side. "Of course he is—and he's a friend of mine," she added.

"Well, get on board right away." Trina gestured toward the landing where a bulbous tram car waited. "You'll be standing next to the windows since you're the last passengers." She was hurrying them both past the gate.

Krista shuddered as she stepped into the car and found herself, as Trina promised, right against the glass. When the door slid shut a minute later, she was so appalled at the descent route that she almost forgot Hamid's presence beside her.

She turned hastily to search for Trina's figure. "I don't want to look at the view . . . somebody else can take my place here. . . ."

"It's too late," Hamid hissed as the car started

to move. "Just stand there quietly! I don't want to attract attention."

As the car swung out into space there was a concerted groan of excitement from the occupants.

"Remember, ladies and gentlemen," Trina babbled happily over the clamor, "we now drop over two thousand feet in six minutes."

Krista paled and closed her eyes. Even Hamid looked around uneasily.

"Today there is a magnificent view of the entire lake—the Alps—the Jura Mountains," Trina droned on. "This is as close to heaven as some of us will ever be."

Or hell, Krista thought as her stomach lurched in sympathy with each jog of the big tram. She stole a furtive look at Hamid and discovered that he was keeping a close watch on her despite their sardine-can existence. Any fleeting hopes she had for a nauseated Moroccan at the next landing stage were instantly dispelled.

"When we arrive at Frakmuntegg approximately three minutes from now," Trina was announcing, "we will leave this tram and board the cable cars going back down to the lake."

Krista muttered to herself, still keeping her eyes closed.

"What did you say?" Hamid asked suspiciously.

"I was merely asking why they don't have any buses or streetcars in this damned country," Krista told him through set teeth. "Once we get off the cable cars, she's probably arranged a helicopter back to the hotel."

"If I were you, I would be wishing for the slowest form of transportation available," he threatened next to her ear. "You can open your eyes now . . . we're almost at the landing. Don't try anything foolish."

"Open your eyes but keep your mouth shut," she repeated bitterly. "It's all right—after this roller coaster, I'm too weak to scream. I wonder if there's a path we can walk down."

"Don't force me to do something I'd regret." He caught her elbow as the tram finally slid to a stop at another concrete landing platform tucked into the side of the mountain. "We'll walk slowly over to that cable car entrance and then we'll request a car by ourselves instead of sharing it."

"Trina won't like that. She's made different arrangements."

His grip tightened and he moved her forward as the tram door was unlocked and opened. "I can convince her. At first, we'll stay with the rest," he murmured softly as the others surged onto the path beside them. "Take it slowly."

Krista kept her head down as she walked dispiritedly on toward the other platform, biting her lip hard as she tried to think. How could she possibly get away from him when they were still halfway up a mountain? Her only chance was to wait and hope that there'd be an opportunity down at the lakeside.

She pulled up in confusion as a group of men suddenly converged around them. Then, without a word being spoken, she felt Hamid's grip yanked from her arm and she saw him being hustled back toward the tramway by three stolid-looking men in neat dark suits. One of them was speaking earnestly into the Moroccan's ear as they half carried him along.

"Now that's a neat maneuver if I ever saw one," said a familiar voice, and Krista whirled to see Jeff Snow standing on one side of her. "Discreet, too," he went on admiringly, speaking over her head to someone on the other side. "Nobody even knew what was happening. You know, I've heard of ostriches hiding their heads in the sand but I'll bet that this is the first time a woman ever kept her eyes closed during the entire Pilatus tour." Jeff's tone changed as he took a closer look at her complexion. He moved hastily forward. "Hang onto her, Ryan! Bless my soul—she's going down for the count."

Chapter *TEN*

Krista dimly felt herself deposited on a convenient wooden bench and struggled to sit upright as her dizziness receded in the access of sudden relief.

"I'm all right," she said in a cross tone. "It was just a combination of that miserable high-wire tram and Hamid's sticking a knife in my side. You know, I think he actually wanted to kill me."

Ryan was standing by the bench staring down at her, a peculiar look on his face. "I know exactly how he felt. Today especially. . . ." He didn't give her a chance to reply but turned to a grinning Jeff and said, "We'd better start down. The weather's getting soupier by the minute."

Jeff craned his neck to peer up at the Pilatus summit. "You're right. Those black clouds are really rolling in. Good thing the cable cars are enclosed." He reached down to give Krista a hand. "Ready to go now?"

She stood up promptly, disdaining his assistance. "Of course. But what about Hamid?"

"What about him?" Ryan wanted to know. "Frankly, I'm happy to see the back of him. He's caused enough trouble."

"Don't I have to prefer charges or something?"

Jeff shook his head. "The Swiss police have that nicely in hand. We'll explain on the way down the mountain. There's plenty of time—the cable ride takes another half hour. Ryan and I can point out

176

the beauty spots on the way as well." He grinned. "We saw them on the way up—or, at least, I did. All your husband could think about was getting to the summit to rescue you."

She raised a skeptical eyebrow. If Ryan was so intent on her safety, why hadn't he been around when she needed him earlier? She stole a covert look at his stony profile as they waited for the next cable car to swing into the terminal for boarding. Strange that he was being so unyielding—from his manner anyone would think she'd been the guilty one. Probably he was one of those men who didn't believe in apologies no matter what he had done. Well, after she'd boarded the train for Rome, he could really enjoy his social life.

"You're looking mighty grim," Jeff chided her. "What's going through that mind of yours now?"

She smiled faintly. "I was just wishing we could walk down. One way or another, I've been up in the air ever since I left home and, frankly, I'm sick of it."

A cable car came clattering into the station and Ryan urged her, none too gently, through its open door. "That's too damned bad! If you want to scramble down the side of Pilatus—do it on your own time. Right now, you look as if you're frozen stiff."

"I'm just turning blue from poor circulation," she told him sweetly. Too sweetly. "Kindly let go of my elbow."

Ryan muttered something under his breath about wishing he could hang onto her neck instead. She calmly ignored that and chose to sit next to Jeff on the seat, making Ryan face them. Then she winced as the door was slammed and the cable car was shoved out into midair on its journey down.

"Don't worry," Jeff assured her quickly. "These things stop rocking after a couple of minutes. Just don't think about it."

Ryan was still scowling at her pale cheeks. "And don't look down—then you won't have to close your eyes." He took an exasperated breath. "Why in the devil did you hare off on this fool excursion, anyway? I could have told you that you wouldn't like it."

She forgot all about the altitude in her anger. "You weren't around to ask. All I heard was that you'd gone out earlier with a strange woman. . . ."

"Strange woman—already?" Jeff was clearly enjoying the discussion. "That wasn't very sporting of you, Ryan. Even the fellows up in the mountains of Morocco kept their wives for twelve months."

"Very funny. Why don't you tell Krista that her 'strange woman' came through the courtesy of the U.S. State Department."

"I'd rather watch you do your own explaining," Jeff began, and then broke off hurriedly. "Ok . . . Ok . . . I get the message." He turned, still laughing, to Krista. "He's right, you know."

"I wish you'd start from the beginning. . . ."

"All right. It will take your mind off the scenery, if nothing else."

"I *like* the scenery." She was peering gingerly through the side window of the gondola as the car went steadily down the hill. "I'm simply tired of having a bird's-eye view of it. It would be just as good from the level."

"For somebody who was in the clutches of a political assassin a few minutes ago, you aren't displaying much curiosity," Jeff complained.

Ryan smiled sardonically. "Go back to the strange woman and watch her ears perk up."

"You can drive around with an entire harem of strange women if . . . ," she began.

Jeff broke into her outburst. "As I was going to say, Ryan called the consulate in Zurich early this morning to explain how Hamid's book had come into your possession. Naturally, they couldn't wait to get a look at it. When they discovered that I was on my way from Geneva, they sent an English-speaking secretary over to bring Ryan in for a powwow."

"I don't understand why they were interested at all," Krista said. "There was a chance that it *was* just a book of proverbs."

Jeff shook his head. "Hamid was well-known in all diplomatic circles by this morning. His disappearance from Morocco had finally hit the foreign papers and the authorities suspected that he'd stolen some restricted documents from the country. The Moroccans have had so much trouble with political extremists lately, that they were understandably nervous about any state secrets getting into the wrong hands."

Krista remembered the roadblocks crisscrossing the country and nodded slowly.

Jeff went on. "All the authorities needed was some tangible evidence to nail Hamid. They kept a close watch on him, but when he was assigned to our tour—he found the perfect 'out' for his stolen data."

"But why did he choose me?" Krista asked, so intent on his story that she forgot to flinch when their cable car rocked going over a pylon.

"Because you were the best of the lot. That's what I explained to your husband earlier. You see, the Westons had traveled extensively in Arabic countries—so Hamid couldn't be sure of *their* loyalties. . . ."

"And Herb?"

He smiled. "Herb's booked for Israel after the Continent. Scarcely an impartial observer in Hamid's eyes."

"I can understand that." She frowned. "What about Eve?"

"Eve's fiancé comes from East Germany and she's reluctant to talk about her life before Vienna." His smile widened. "The only ones who were lily-white . . . beyond suspicion . . . were Dr. Talbot and . . ."

"And the obliging Mrs. Talbot," Ryan put in.

"Exactly. Hamid put the evidence with you, suspecting that Krista would take especially good care of it. By then, he discovered the authorities had caught wind of his activities and he couldn't chance being searched at that first unexpected roadblock. He had to get his plans—and you—out of the country. The sooner the better. Probably he'd planned his own escape long ago."

"That's why he wanted to know about our stay in Basel." Krista was thinking back. "And I suppose the friend's name he gave was just another precaution. . . ."

Jeff tried to settle more comfortably on the narrow bench. "That's right. In case he couldn't pick up the book in person."

"I wonder how he found out we were in Lucerne."

Ryan raised his glance from the green meadows below them to her intent profile. "That stumped me, too—until I remembered that the desk clerk called the hotel in Basel saying we'd been delayed. Probably Hamid hopped a train right away."

"That's what we suspect," Jeff said. He turned back to Krista. "Ryan practically had it confirmed when he called the hotel about noon. He missed you, but an obliging hotel porter said he'd just seen you off on the Pilatus launch, and there was a man of Hamid's description who'd been in the hotel earlier asking about the Talbots."

"But Hamid wasn't on the launch with me," she protested.

"There's a train that goes directly to the cog railway terminus," Ryan told her. "All he had to do was wait for you to arrive in the launch and then follow you up the mountain."

"Something we tried to do, incidentally," Jeff offered. "Only we were twenty minutes behind Hamid. By the time Ryan and I collected those three Swiss policemen, we had to come up this side by cable car and hope to intercept you."

Krista thought of those moments on the summit of the mountain when she wondered whether Hamid would allow her descent and shuddered visibly.

Ryan saw her troubled expression. "That's enough of the explanations for now," he told Jeff. "Krista has had all she can take."

Even though she was still angry with him, she was grateful for his defense. "I *would* like to forget it. Is somebody else taking care of that darned book?"

Jeff chuckled. "You bet! Too bad you didn't put it up for grabs. You would have had half the crooks in this part of the world bidding on it."

"But why didn't the Swiss just stop Hamid at their border when he tried to enter the country?" Ryan asked.

"They couldn't. The Swiss have given up border checks. No passport controls for visitors. It's their new policy, but it backfired in this case. Don't worry—they'll march him to the next plane leaving the country and make sure he gets on it."

"And the book?" Krista asked.

"Leave that to the diplomats," Jeff said. "At least the information didn't get to a bunch of extremists who were just waiting to fire the torch." He glanced through the window beside him. "It's a pity the sun's still under the clouds—we're coming down into the alpine farms now."

Krista peered out on her side, her fears completely forgotten. Even Ryan's expression relaxed as they admired the picturesque chalets in the mountain meadows below them. Pink and yellow wildflowers grew in attractive clusters at the fenced boundaries providing touches of color against the green pasture grasses. Sturdy Brown Swiss cattle grazed peacefully, ignoring the moving chain of cable cars above their heads.

"Very difficult to get cows for these alpine farms," Jeff informed Krista. "The mountain people have to pay a premium for the breed."

"Why is that? Do they need a hardy stock for the mountain pastures?"

Ryan glanced at Jeff's expression and then laughed. "Wait for it, Krista. He's about to explain how they have to search for cattle with short legs on one side to stand on the hillsides."

"Oh, no! That joke had ivy on it when I was growing up."

Jeff shrugged at her pained look. "Well, I deserve something after chasing you all over Switzerland. If there were any more taxpayers like you, Mrs. Talbot, I'd demand a raise in salary." Then, as he saw the landing platform for the cable station in the distance, he added, "Don't forget, Ryan—you promised to tour me through the zoo in Basel tomorrow. I want to see those apes you were talking about. There's a congressman back home who's a dead ringer for a baboon. . . ." He broke off sheepishly. "Sorry—now you can see why I'm not a career diplomat."

Krista patted his hand. "Well, Superman couldn't have looked more welcome up there on the side of the mountain."

"Better give your husband part of the credit. If he hadn't brought that book around in the first place ..." He stopped as Ryan stirred restlessly. "Anyhow ... it's over now. You two can take the car that's waiting for us. I'll hang around and see what the Swiss authorities have to say." He stood up as their cable car swung to a stop and an attendant opened the door. "Here we are—safe and sound, Krista. Now you can relax."

She smiled wryly at his blithe comment. One look at Ryan's tight jaw as she filed beside him down the ramp in a light drizzle of rain was enough to convince her that the really dangerous part of the day was yet to come.

Ryan obviously felt the same way. He maintained an aloof silence in the car on their trip back to the hotel. This time they were chauffeured by an elderly Swiss gentleman who took one look at their stony faces and drove back to Lucerne by the shortest possible route. He remained discreetly silent as they climbed out at the hotel. All in all, Krista decided, the Talbots were't doing much to improve American-Swiss relations.

The situation didn't change as they entered the lobby.

She tried to protest as Ryan marched her directly to the marble stairs. "I have to stop and see the hall porter. He's getting some tickets for me."

Ryan didn't slacken pace. "The hell he is."

She almost stumbled at his unexpected response. "Will you let go of my arm?" she hissed.

"I tell you—he's reserved a train ticket to Rome for me. I saw him this morning."

"And I canceled it when I talked to him on the telephone a few minutes later."

"But my luggage . . ." She was breathless as he pulled her past the second landing on the wide stairway. "He was going to store it for me."

"It never left the room." Ryan didn't even look at her. "I told him you'd changed your plans."

"But I haven't changed them!"

"That's what you think." He yanked her down the corridor like an unwelcome appendage until he came to a halt in front of their door. He unlocked it, pushed her inside, and slammed it behind them.

She rounded on him fiercely. "If you think this antediluvian display is going to make any difference, you're crazy." Her voice wavered despite her determination to keep it steady. "How you can have the almighty nerve to adopt such a high-handed attitude after the way you acted . . ."

Ryan wasn't listening. He was storming back at her. "You're in a hell of a spot to complain about anyone being high-handed. . . ."

"Treating me as if I were a six-year-old as you dragged me through the lobby." Her anger was sheer relief after a day of frozen despair. "Everybody was staring at us. What will people think?"

Ryan expressed his opinion of what people thought in six succinct words and then went on pithily. "It's damned lucky for you, you're not six years old or I'd have done worse. To run off like that . . . after last night. . . ."

Tears were streaming unnoticed down Krista's cheeks at the same time she was saying, "How could you go off like that . . . after last night. . . ."

As their words clashed, both of them fell silent,

uncertainty and bewilderment chasing the bad temper from their faces.

Krista shivered as they faced each other in the narrow entrance hall. It was nervous reaction as much as anything else but Ryan interpreted it differently.

He jerked his head toward the bedroom. "You better change. There's no sense getting a chill from wet clothes." His voice was regaining its normal cadence, as if he'd leashed his anger for the moment.

Krista accepted the olive branch for what it was worth. "All right." She rubbed the tears from her cheeks with the back of her hand, awkwardly. "But you'd better change, too. You got soaked getting into the hotel." She gestured toward the raindrops still visible on his sport coat.

He nodded, pulling a clean handkerchief from his pocket as he followed her into the other room. "Here—take this."

"Thank you." She accepted it gratefully and blew her nose. It was hard to sound dignified when she had to sniffle every three seconds.

Ryan stared at her a minute longer and then went over to get a hanger before shrugging out of his wet coat. Krista followed his example and stared with dismay at the wet patches on her suede topcoat.

She turned to intercept Ryan's glance once again as he stood by the bed calmly unbuttoning his shirt. "Now that we've both calmed down a little bit," he began awkwardly, "maybe we could sort things out."

"Yes?" She made a production out of putting her coat on the hanger, unable to sustain that suddenly searching look.

"Why *did* you run out on me, Kris?" His tone

was quiet. "Didn't last night mean anything to you?"

"Of *course* it did." There was no doubting the sincerity of her reply. "That's why it hurt so much to find you'd gone off without a word this morning. Oh, I know that you hadn't made any real commitments—and I realize now that the woman who met you was strictly business—but you could at least have told me." She stopped at his abrupt gesture. "Now, what's the matter?"

"I could ask you the same thing. What's wrong with leaving a note? I *told* you I'd call as soon as I found out anything and to stick around the hotel." At her blank look, he persisted: "In the note I left on the newspaper. I wrote on the margin next to that article about Hamid's disappearance from Morocco. The one that told how he was a suspected political extremist. . . ."

"But I didn't even *see* the paper," she wailed. "How was I to know?"

"Well—why do you think I took that book to the consulate in the first place?" There was anger in his tone again, but this time it merely fired a glow of happiness on her incredulous face. "*Will* you hang up that coat," he ordered her finally. "If you're not going to wear it, there's no point in clutching it all day."

She obeyed him but stayed next to the armoire door as if needing its support as she tried to remember. "I know now," she said at length. "The maid took that paper out with your breakfast tray. When my breakfast came, they'd given me a brand-new one."

"You thought I'd just walked out?" He was astounded. "That I didn't want to be with you— even after last night?"

She nodded meekly, unable to meet his eyes.

"My God, woman . . ." There was a definite undercurrent of laughter in his voice now. "Damned if you don't take a lot of convincing. I was so tired this morning that I yawned all the way to the police station."

Krista felt the flush on her cheeks spread slowly. "Well, you didn't say anything about ... about loving me." The last words came out with difficulty.

He stayed quietly by the bed. "Honey, I've been loving you so long that I ache with it." He watched her head come up at that and smiled gently. "I was in trouble the first time I saw you. I should have slammed the office door the day you applied for a job. Instead I dreamed up one and even arranged to share an office with you." His mouth twisted. "Unfortunately, that's when everything came to a screeching halt. I couldn't get any closer to you than the edge of your desk."

"Ryan—you didn't try."

"The hell I didn't. You just weren't looking. The only things that got your attention had four legs, slept in incubators, and had to be fed every three hours. I was getting desperate when this trip came up."

"You mean this whole thing was planned?" Her voice rose incredulously. "Was Dr. Baldwin in on it, too?"

His grin widened. "Well, he was happy to co-operate. He said it was time to put me out of my misery. Incidentally, we have an invitation to dinner with them the night we get home."

She could scarcely believe it. "But he didn't let on at all! To think he was scheming like a marriage broker . . ."

"*We* were scheming." Ryan waited for a peal of thunder to subside as the rain outside their windows turned into an early summer storm. "The marriage requirement for this tour was a final desperate stroke. And a lot of good it did. . . ." He turned to the bed table and started emptying his pockets. "You'd barely signed the marriage license when you put on an armor a foot thick."

She stood staring at him while he calmly deposited his change and cigarettes on the glass-topped table. Did he have to be so matter-of-fact about everything, she wondered. Surely he could wait to change his clothes.

Then she saw by his tense profile that he *was* waiting. That he wasn't sure of her response . . . even now.

Suddenly she recalled that she hadn't been generous with her declarations of love last night either. Evidently he'd mistaken shyness for a lack of feeling. "Oh, Ryan! What fools we've been!" She stretched out her hands as she went to him, forgetting her pride in a desire to make things right. "I love you, too. Why do you think I said 'yes' in the first place? I just put on that armor because I was scared to death. I have been ever since I said . . . 'I do.' You talked so much about 'sensible' platonic marriages that I was afraid to act normal for fear you'd run in the other direction." She moved her hands over the strong muscles on his chest and let them curve around his neck. "When you finally put an end to our foolishness last night, I wanted to shout with happiness."

Ryan didn't say anything. There was no necessity for it. His expression of relief and joy was an open avowal of his love.

Then slowly he came to life. She felt his hands at her hips, pulling her close to him. As he bent to kiss her parted lips, she trembled suddenly with excitement. A few minutes later, she was trembling for an entirely different reason and it was obvious that Ryan felt the same way.

She pulled back an inch or so—postponing the final miracle because she still couldn't believe her luck. A peal of thunder sounded overhead—reminding her of last night.

Deliberately she met Ryan's glance. She had difficulty steadying her voice but there was a provocative spark in it as she confessed, "When I was young and there was a storm like this—I always went right to bed and buried my head under the covers.

"Is that so?" Ryan's shoulders moved with silent laughter as he bent and lifted her purposefully in his arms. "I know a way," he said, "to improve on the therapy."

SIGNET Romances You'll Enjoy

☐ **WHO IS LUCINDA? by Hermina Black.** Her past was buried in memory. Could she trust this new love that wanted to claim her future? (#T5809—75¢)

☐ **THE RED LADY by Katharine Newlin Burt.** Janice's world tenses with suspense and high passion as she tries to free herself from threatening evil and to prove her innocence to the one man she longs to love. . . . (#T5670—75¢)

☐ **THE RAINBOW CHASERS (Condensed for Modern Readers) by Marion Naismith.** When David Lorimer appeared in the village, Louise found herself yearning for his love. But how could she trust her heart to a man whose past was shrouded in mystery . . . ? (#P5621—60¢)

☐ **LOVE ON A HOLIDAY (originally entitled Alison Comes Home) by I. Torr.** Could Ken Macgregor protect Alison from the unknown terror that was about to engulf her? (#P5620—60¢)

☐ **ROYAL SCOT by Vivian Donald.** It began as a battle to restore the Scottish monarchy and ended in love and a flight to the heather. (#P5181—60¢)

☐ **SECRETS CAN BE FATAL by Monica Heath.** A lovely young girl accompanies a writer to a deserted mansion to work with him on his next book, not realizing that the bizarre tale he is weaving is really the story of her own past, a past she has never known. (#P5180—60¢)

THE NEW AMERICAN LIBRARY, INC.,
P.O. Box 999, Bergenfield, New Jersey 07621

Please send me the SIGNET BOOKS I have checked above. I am enclosing $_____(check or money order—no currency or C.O.D.'s). Please include the list price plus 25¢ a copy to cover handling and mailing costs. (Prices and numbers are subject to change without notice.)

Name_____

Address_____

City_____State_____Zip Code_____
Allow at least 3 weeks for delivery

Bestsellers from SIGNET

☐ **BRING ME A UNICORN: The Diaries and Letters of Anne Morrow Lindbergh (1922–1928) by Anne Morrow Lindbergh.** Imagine being loved by the most worshipped hero on Earth. This nationally acclaimed bestseller is the chronicle of just such a love. The hero was Charles Lindbergh; the woman he loved was Anne Morrow Lindbergh; and the story of their love was one of the greatest romances of any time. "Extraordinary . . . brings to intense life every moment as she lived it."—New York Times Book Review   (#W5352—$1.50)

☐ **ELEANOR AND FRANKLIN by Joseph P. Lash.** Foreword by Arthur M. Schlesinger, Jr. A number 1 bestseller and winner of the Pulitzer Prize and the National Book Award, this is the intimate chronicle of Eleanor Roosevelt and her marriage to Franklin D. Roosevelt, with its painful secrets and public triumphs. "An exceptionally candid, exhaustive . . . heartrending book."—The New Yorker   (#J5310—$1.95)

☐ **JENNIE, VOLUME I: The Life of Lady Randolph Churchill by Ralph G. Martin.** In JENNIE, Ralph G. Martin creates a vivid picture of an exciting woman, Lady Randolph Churchill, who was the mother of perhaps the greatest statesman of this century, Winston Churchill, and in her own right, one of the most colorful and fascinating women of the Victorian era.   (#E5229—$1.75)

☐ **JENNIE, VOLUME II: The Life of Lady Randolph Churchill, the Dramatic Years 1895–1921 by Ralph G. Martin.** The climactic years of scandalous passion and immortal greatness of the American beauty who raised a son to shape history, Winston Churchill. "An extraordinary lady . . . if you couldn't put down JENNIE ONE, you'll find JENNIE TWO just as compulsive reading!"—Washington Post   (#E5196—$1.75)

THE NEW AMERICAN LIBRARY, INC.,
P.O. Box 999, Bergenfield, New Jersey 07621

Please send me the SIGNET BOOKS I have checked above. I am enclosing $_____(check or money order—no currency or C.O.D.'s). Please include the list price plus 25¢ a copy to cover handling and mailing costs. (Prices and numbers are subject to change without notice.)

Name_____

Address_____

City_____State_____Zip Code_____
Allow at least 3 weeks for delivery